MW00978273

DREAMCATCHER

Pamela Kavanagh

DREAMCATCHER

Cover and inside illustrations: © 2008 Jennifer Bell
Cover layout: Stabenfeldt A/S

Typeset by Roberta L. Melzl
Editor: Bobbie Chase
Printed in Germany, 2008

ISBN: 978-1-933343-86-0

Available exclusively through PONY Book Club.

PROLOGUE

The tracks came snaking down the hillside behind the farm, a clear churning of hooves and wheels on the rutted pathway known as the old lane.

I studied them, puzzled. They seemed to belong to a lightweight horse and buggy – the kind seen at shows that make you drool with envy, all high-stepping horseflesh and glossy paintwork and shiny black harness – not the plodding progress of Connor's two heavyweight Shires with their cumbersome log cart. What's more, they had not been here a minute ago when I had let out the hens... my responsibility during summer vacation, which I was spending here at Cross Hill while Mom and Eddie were touring with the jazz band.

Nor had I heard a horse-drawn vehicle go by. So how had the tracks gotten here?

Standing there in the hazy morning sunshine, I felt a creeping chill, as if an unseen wintry hand had been waved, spreading an aching coldness that I, in my innocence, put down to my troubled state of mind. Life had turned upside down lately, what with my parents' divorce and Mom marrying Eddie. Then again, I had gained a grown-up stepbrother and a great place to come on visits. I envied Connor his hilly retreat where he did forestry work with the horses, tended the sheep with Gyp the collie, and where the days had stability and purpose. I think Connor had done his best to make me feel at home by giving me the poultry to

5

care for and other tasks to do, but even here at Cross Hill I had the same sense of being... well, not a misfit exactly, but not really fitting in either. I was still *bookworm Tessa with her plain unremarkable looks and passion for ponies*.

As I gazed at those strange prints, fragments of the dream I'd had every night since arriving at Cross Hill came back to me. The tantalizing throb of hoofbeats. The horse whinnying to the morning... his warm, grassy smell as he put his soft muzzle in my palm. All at once I wanted to catch that dream and make it reality. Mom could have her amazing singing voice and Eddie was welcome to his flare for the tenor sax. Connor could keep his refuge in the hills. I, Tessa Darcy, wanted something different; I wanted the horse that lived in my dreams.

CHAPTER ONE

"Tessa?" hollered Connor from the stables. "Give me a hand here, will you?"

His shout was echoed by an impatient clop and the scrape of hooves on the stone floor of the stalls. After taking the basket of newly laid eggs into the kitchen, I hurried across the farmyard and entered the old-fashioned stable with its four high-sided stalls and central aisle where big black Polly stood already harnessed and waiting.

Connor was tacking up the smaller bay in the first stall. Tallish, dark-haired and musclular, Connor was a younger version of his father, except that where Eddie's fitness came from work-outs at the gym, Connor's was from physical, hard work. And where Eddie smiled easily, Connor did not.

"Ah, there you are," he said, without stopping what he was doing. "Grab Bassy's traces for me, will you, Tessa? They're on the hook over there by the window."

I did so, my mind still on those curious tracks that seemed to have appeared out of nowhere. "Connor, have you seen a pony and trap go by? I just noticed some hoof and wheel marks on that sandy lane. Don't know how they got there."

"What?" He glanced up, a faintly startled look in his flint-gray eyes, and then he shrugged. "You must be mistaken. That's just an old cattle driver's road that goes down to the village. At one time people herded their farm-stock along it to trade in the market. Nobody uses it much these days."

"Somebody does. The tracks are there. Come and see."

"Not now, Tessa. I'm late as it is," Connor said, going decisively back to dealing with the buckles and straps. "I should be finished in the woods today. Are you coming with me?"

"I'm not sure."

I was left with the distinct feeling of being put off. It was fun helping in the forest, where the densely wooded slopes made access for mechanized vehicles impossible and only horses could make it through. But those tracks intrigued me. I had to see where they led.

"I don't like leaving you here on your own," Connor said.

"Why not? I'm not a child. I'll be fifteen soon."

"Is that right?" He sounded amused. "So what are your plans, old lady?"

"I might go for a walk. Explore a little."

"Then you'd better take the dog with you. I won't need the two horses tomorrow. You can have Bassy if you like."

"Great." I'd already been up on Bassy, the Shire. Broad-backed and slow, he was not the most interesting ride but any horse was better than none. "Thanks, Connor."

"No problem."

Delving into a tack box on the ledge, he seized a grooming cloth and went through his usual ritual of buffing up the decorative forehead brass on the blinkered driving bridle so that it gleamed dully in the dimness of the building. The brass was what Connor called a "flash," a simple disc that had none of the appeal of the crescent moons and wheat-sheaves that adorned the fireplace of the farmhouse kitchen. Polly's headpiece, I noticed, was equally plain.

8

"I don't know why you bother with those brass pieces," I said idly. "They're boring. And it's a pain cleaning them."

"Let's just call it tradition," Connor replied in a way that put an end to the matter.

Saying he'd be back by lunchtime, he clicked his tongue to the horses and led them out to hitch them to the cart. Soon afterwards they went rumbling down the road, the horses high-stepping boldly, Connor sitting hunched on the driving seat, his woodman's tools beside him. I gazed after him, at a loss to know why he'd been so curt with me. Putting it down to his haste to be gone, I headed for the house.

Cross Hill farmhouse was square and stone-built, with deep-set windows, solid doors and tall chimneys, the nearest puffing a spiral of blue smoke from the kitchen wood-burning stove that heated the water, cooked the meals and warmed weak newborn lambs in springtime. Uneven flagstoned floors tripped the unwary, and the age-blackened ceiling beams gave little head clearance, often catching Connor, even though he, like generations of Boyds before him, had been born here and should have been used to it. As well as the big cluttered kitchen where everything happened, there were three other downstairs rooms where nothing much did. One held an upright piano, the top piled with well-thumbed sheet music, mostly jazz.

My bedroom was accessed from the kitchen by a twisting back stair and looked out over the farmyard and the steep hillside beyond. It had a sloped ceiling, a planked floor with a cozy sheepskin rug by the bed, and furniture of mellowed pine.

Wanting my wallet, as I needed postage stamps from the village, I went to get it and paused in front of the mirror. Clear hazel eyes gazed back at me from what Dad had called a healthy face. My short light-brown hair with bangs was glossy and straight, my chin stubborn and mouth set. Grimacing at myself, I grabbed my wallet, rejected the cell phone next to it – useless, since the signal was bad up here in the hills – and went running back downstairs again.

Gyp was snoozing by the kitchen stove, a huddle of black and white fur, but glanced up hopefully when I appeared.

"Come on, boy." I took down his leash from the peg by the back door. "Walk time!"

Outside, the dewy ground steamed in the growing warmth of the sun. The tracks stood out clearly and off we went, trailing them downhill, Gyp lagging a little, as if he knew better than to follow mere wheel marks on the path.

Larks soared and sang overhead and the mingled scents of grass and peaty earth were strong in the air. Sometimes the prints were lost where the surface was firmer, but they were always just ahead, urging me on. We jumped the streams that trickled across our path, sloshing through the soggier parts. Passing through a patch of woodland, the gnarled old oaks and younger mountain ashes forming a leafy canopy above, we came out again between steep-sided banks where rabbits bolted for cover.

The tracks were still here, rolling along the sunken lane which gradually gave way to open hillside. Below me, at the head of the valley, a small cottage and stable yard gleamed with new paint. The property was surrounded by neatly fenced grassy paddocks and training areas, one with show jumps and what looked like a schooling ring with markers. Further on was the silver glint of the river as it rushed through the village of Rydale, the summer haunt of canoeists and vacationers.

Eventually the rutted lane petered out and became the

solid asphalt of the village road, with its passing cars and an occasional tractor or horse trailer. Following it a short distance, we arrived at the cottage I'd noticed from above, the front brightened by window boxes and tubs of summer flowers. Above the oak-stained front door swung a sign that read *The Old Forge* in bold black letters.

In contrast to the carefully restored living quarters, a section on the end that must once have been the smithy, or blacksmith's shop, had not been touched and remained in its original rough-and-ready state. It looked long closed down, the wide doors and narrow windows securely boarded over with stout planking that had weathered to a nondescript sludge color.

I was standing there with Gyp, contemplating the crumbling damp-patched walls and pitched roof, wondering why it had been left in such disrepair, when a boy appeared around the side of the cottage. He looked older than I; around sixteen or seventeen, and judging from his mucky boots, the straw sticking to his polo shirt and everyday jodhpurs, he had come straight from the stables.

"Hi," he greeted me, coming up to pet Gyp. "Nice dog you've got there."

"Yes, he's great. He's not mine – though I wish he was!"

The boy smiled, a nice quirky sort of smile that went with his laughing blue eyes and untidy mop of glossy brown hair. "My name's Nick Meredith. I don't think I've seen you around before."

"No, I'm new here," I told him. "I'm Tessa Darcy and this is Gyp. We're from Cross Hill Farm."

"Really? That's Connor Boyd's place. We get our hay from there. He has draft horses, right?"

"Yes, two of them. You must be the owner of the pony and trap. We followed your tracks down the old lane."

The smile vanished. "You couldn't have," Nick said. "I don't do carriage driving."

"But the tracks are there," I said indignantly. "They led here."

"Is that right? Something else must have made them. The hills are kind of steep here for ponies and traps. They're good for riding, though. Do you ride?"

Baffled, for this was the second time today I'd blanked on what seemed a perfectly ordinary situation, I said I did and the smile returned, quirkier than ever.

"Great. Want to come and meet the horses? You'd better say hello to my sister first. You can bring Gyp. She'll love him."

Nick led the way around to the back of the cottage and across a small courtyard with lawn chairs and more tubs of flowers. The kitchen door was propped open to the summer day. On the step, a fluffy tortoiseshell cat sat washing itself in the sunshine.

"That's Tishy," Nick said. "She's Lucy's cat. This way."

With Gyp in tow I followed him inside to the smell of new paint and a cheerful mish-mash of stuccoed walls, country style furnishings and a definite flare for handicrafts. We went through to a room that Nick called the den, where a spinning wheel stood in a corner and skeins of wool in rainbow colors hung from the ceiling beams. Wicker baskets were everywhere, filled with balls of yarn speared with knitting needles.

At a table, a young woman sat engrossed in a glossy brochure featuring what looked like shop equipment and accessories. She was dressed in a chambray skirt paired with a plain white T-shirt and wore her long tawny-gold hair in a loose braid that fell casually over her shoulder. Glancing up, she smiled enquiringly.

Nick made the introductions. "Lucy, meet Tessa Darcy and Gyp. Tessa, this is my sister Lucy."

"Hello, Tessa," Lucy said. She was incredibly pretty, with eyes the same sparkling blue as her brother's. "Are you here on vacation?"

"Sort of. My Mom and step-dad – I call him Eddie – have gone on tour with a jazz band so I'm staying at the farm with Connor."

Recognition blazed on both faces. "The Eddie Boyd Band?" Nick said with delight. "So your Mom must be Vanessa Darcy – wow!"

"Don't mind Nick!" Lucy looked wry. "He's jazz crazy. I must admit I'm a Vanessa Darcy fan myself. Her voice is really something. And she's got such style."

"Yes," I said, quietly. It was my misfortune to have taken after my mild unassuming father rather than my glamorous extrovert mother. Dad, not one to make a fuss, had taken off, right out of our lives, after the split. I adored my dad and longed to hear from him. For ages I had waited for word, anything to know that he was all right and missing me as much as I missed him. But the weeks had become months and no word had come.

Lucy said, "We knew Eddie Boyd was a local celebrity, though we've never met him. Connor's a lot like his dad, isn't he?"

"Only in looks. Connor's quieter and can be a little grumpy. We get along okay, though. His mother died when he was little and Eddie brought him up. Eddie was farming at Cross Hill then, until the jazz band took off. That's when he met Mom. Connor's not into show business. He likes the farm and the horses."

"Sensible guy," said Nick.

While we were talking Nick had gone to the kitchen and returned with a large jug of homemade lemonade and tall glasses on a tray. Lucy produced some chocolate chip cookies from a cupboard and we all sat down to the feast on the table. Nibbling a cookie, Gyp at my feet, I heard how the Merediths came to live here. It was nothing new to me. Professional parents heavily involved with their careers, Grandmother more or less bringing up the children, leaving them everything when she passed away.

"Lucy was independent by then," Nick said. "Mom and Dad were living overseas. We looked for affordable properties on the Internet and this place suited us. We liked Rydale immediately. Our idea was to turn the smithy into a craft shop, but it hasn't happened yet."

"Well, there have been problems." Other words hovered on Lucy's lips, but then she gave a little shrugging smile and said, "I want to stock locally made crafts as well as the usual merchandise. I saw some fantastic woodcuts of horses the other day. The man from the General Store makes them. I think they're very marketable."

"It's just a small matter of getting the interest," Nick added in disparaging mutter.

"It'll come." Lucy darted him a cautionary glance. "We must be patient."

Glancing from one to the other, trying to figure out what was wrong, my attention was caught by a gossamer shawl draped on the back of a chair, and it struck a chord.

"Lucy Meredith fashions! Of course! You're the label on those fantastic shawls and scarves! Mom's crazy about them."

"Is she?" Lucy looked pleased. "Well!"

"Told you," Nick said to his sister. "You'd be better sticking with your designer stuff and forgetting about the craft business. I'd have thought a workshop in the city was enough for anyone."

"But we're here now," Lucy pointed out gently. "We've got the planning permit. Besides, branching out is what I want to do. It's my dream."

"Like mine's eventing." Nick stood up. "Let's forget all this. Come and see my two hopefuls. Gyp can stay here with Lucy. She and equines don't exactly mix."

Leaving Lucy to her brochures, I went with Nick out to the stable yard and met the two horses, Sea Holly and Rough Tweed.

"This is Tweed," Nick said proudly, rubbing the big horse's forehead, pulling his long ears. He was around seventeen hands, a solidly built liver chestnut with a plain head and plenty of meat on his bones. "He's seven now, and getting better all the time. He's great at cross country and in the jumping ring, but his dressage needs work."

"Oh well, you can't have everything." Envious, I patted Rough Tweed's solid neck. "Where do you go for some cross-country experience?"

"I've been lucky there. The farmer whose land borders ours lets me use his fields. I helped with the harvest so he's returning the favor." Nick offered the big horse a slice of carrot, which he chomped avidly. "Tweed's true-blue. A best friend kind of horse. When he's out in the field he always comes running up to the gate to talk to me. Sea Holly's more reserved. Come and see."

In the next stall, Sea Holly put her pretty head over the door and nickered for attention. She was a youthful dappled gray and looked smaller than Tweed, finer boned and very feminine. "She's over seventeen hands, though you wouldn't think it. She's six now, and better on the dressage

16

front than Tweed but not as bold across country. I haven't had her long. A girl I know told me she was for sale and I went to try her. I liked her at once. She moves well and she's comfortable to ride. I'm not really worried about her performance over the fences. She's got time yet."

"Are they entered in any competitions?" I asked.

"We've got one coming up in August. A one-day event qualifier. If we get through that they'll move up to the next level. Here's hoping."

A loud banging noise and a piercing whinny from the opposite stall made me look up. Nick grinned his lopsided grin. "That's my big mistake."

"Why do you say that?"

"Because he is. I've only had that one a couple of weeks. We went to the auction and got taken. Well, he was cheap and I thought there was something about him. He's only four. Want to see?"

The horse was stabled at the end of a row of stalls in what had once been a partitioned stallion stall, the type with iron rails and a double lock on the door. He was a tall, slender roan, not blue or strawberry but somewhere in between, with an unruly mane and tail, a small dished head and an uncompromising expression. At first glance I felt a crushing disappointment. This animal was not in the same class as the other two. And then I looked again... at his nice short back, his long clean legs, his well-proportioned neck and sloped shoulder and rounded quarters.

"Hello, boy," I murmured, entering the stall with my hand outstretched. The horse dipped his soft muzzle into my palm and blew gently. Then he looked straight at me as if to say, *Come on, climb aboard and let's go!*

Incredible intelligence and humor were evident in those

17

eyes. This was a thinking horse; not the easiest to manage and capable of tricks at every turn. But I gazed and gazed at him, knowing I had found my dream.

The roan gave a huge sneezing snort and began to rub his bony head up and down my body, leaving grease marks all over my jeans and pale pink top. Laughing, I patted him, whispering nonsense, telling him how great he was and how I'd love to ride him,

"Hey, he likes you!" said Nick from the railed door. "He does! He really likes you!"

I'd almost forgotten Nick existed and looked up, puzzled. "What do you mean? Why shouldn't he like someone?"

"Because he's not the friendliest creature. He sank his teeth into my sister's arm before he'd been here two minutes. It's no wonder she doesn't like horses. He threw me as soon as I got up on him."

"He could have felt strange. Maybe he needed to settle in a bit first."

"Maybe," Nick echoed without much faith. "Our problem is time. There hasn't been much to spare, though it's better now that it's summer vacation. I still have to put in the work with the other two, and I'm ashamed to say this one gets left out." That was when he uttered the magical words. "You can try him if you like. Come tomorrow. Bring your hard hat." He looked suddenly doubtful. "He's no novice ride."

"That's okay," I said.

Fortunately, my mom might not be the cuddly sort of mother, but she's wonderful in other ways. At the riding center where I spent all my spare time I'd had the best instruction money could buy. I had a wiry strength and determination. No horse got the better of me if I could help it. You have to read their minds and find out what makes them tick. They're all different, and all wonderful; the best creatures on earth.

I kept on fussing over the speckled roan, peering at Nick through the tangle of unkempt mane. "I'd love to ride him. Is it all right if I come over on Bassy? He's one of Connor's Shires."

"That's fine. We'll find a stall for him while you try Sunny out."

"Sunny?" I made a face. "Ugh, is that what you named him?"

"I call them all that until a more suitable name occurs to me, which hasn't happened yet with this guy."

I caught my breath. I knew the perfect name for this horse. "How about Dreamcatcher?"

Nick gave a dispassionate shrug, as if he had already written the animal off. "Dreamcatcher it is."

After a while I collected Gyp and we walked on to the village. At the General Store I bought the stamps and added the biggest pack of chocolate bars in the shop.

"Low on energy?" remarked the woman at the register cheerfully.

"Just addicted. Mom says too much sweet stuff gives you acne, but it doesn't seem to with me."

"That's good. You wouldn't want to spoil that lovely complexion." The woman folded her arms, all set for a chat. "You must be from Cross Hill… I recognized the dog. Gyp, isn't it? You've had a long walk."

"Yes, it certainly was."

She seemed friendly and I told her about Mom and what I was doing here in Rydale. The woman listened, nodding and smiling – until I mentioned where I had just come from. Her brows snapped together in a frown.

"The Old Forge!" she muttered. "It should never have been sold. Places like that are best left alone till they're gone and forgotten."

I was about to ask her what she meant, but the moment was lost when the door burst open to admit a rowdy crowd of canoeists so I said goodbye and left.

Walking slowly back through the pretty riverside resort, I dove into the chocolate, and pondered what the woman had said. Other things sprang to mind. Nick's – and Connor's, come to think of it – evasiveness over the tracks on the lane. Lucy's remark about the craft shop venture.

It'll come. We must be patient.

What had she meant? Why the guarded words, the strained glances? The same look had crossed the shop assistant's face just now. It had been almost fearful. What had happened at the Old Forge to stir such feelings?

It was almost noon, and remembering that Connor was due home for lunch, I gave Gyp's leash a tug and quickened my step. On reaching the lane, I froze – the deep imprints of iron-shod hooves and wheels, that had been all too obvious only a couple of hours ago, were now gone without a trace!

CHAPTER TWO

I didn't dwell on the puzzle of the vanishing prints, at least not right away. There had to be a rational explanation, such as the high ground being wet after the night and the marks dissolving as the sun dried everything up. Anyway, I was thinking about tomorrow and riding Dreamcatcher.

"Just be careful," Connor cautioned. "I know you're an ace jockey, future Olympic star and so on. But I'll have Vanessa to answer to if you end up in a cast."

"Oh, be quiet!" I said, secretly pleased at Connor's backhanded praise of my riding ability. He was wrong about the Olympic part, though. I was only competitive with myself. At school I had to get top grades in everything or I was miserable, and it was the same with horses. My motto is do it, and do it well. But as far as competition work? I couldn't! I could never tackle the eventing circuit like Nick. My nerves would be shot. "Mom doesn't fuss over what I ride, so why should you? Dreamcatcher's a great horse, Connor," I finished passionately.

Connor actually smiled, his sun-browned face crinkling up. "Aren't they all! Okay. Go and ride your pony. It'll be a busy day for me tomorrow, so I won't be back till late."

"Same here," I countered gleefully, and ran upstairs to put out some jodhpurs and a clean shirt for the next day.

That evening when I checked the computer for emails there were two from Mom. The opening gig had been a huge success, she said. Mom sent her regards to Connor and asked if there was anything I needed.

My mind slid longingly to Dreamcatcher and away again. We had been through this many times before. Our lifestyle did not lend itself to horse ownership. Where would we keep it? Home was a spacious apartment in the heart of a big city, with not even a garden, never mind the necessary stabling and field. Stabling was out of the question. There wasn't a horse facility within traveling distance and besides, I just wasn't interested in not having my animal with me at all times.

So I replied that I was fine, Connor was fine, and that I was glad the tour was off to a good start, and left it at that. I knew that Connor's messages to his dad dealt mostly with farm issues and some problems regarding the house and buildings. Maintaining a property as old as Cross Hill was never easy.

I wanted, badly, to ask Mom if she'd heard from Dad but decided against it. She would only have worried that I was missing him, and right now her main focus had to be the tour. Dad would have understood about Dreamcatcher. He had ridden as a boy and had kept his interest in horses.

Drat you, Dad, I thought, giving the send button a savage jab that sent Mom's message spinning off into cyberspace. Why don't you get in touch? Don't you care about me any more? I bit my lip, knowing this was not the case. Dad, annoyingly vague but immensely kind, would very likely be stowed away at some misty-towered university, writing a paper on a subject that totally absorbed him. This tendency to remove himself emotionally from the everyday world, as well as a frustrating lack of concern for his health and the eye trouble that sometimes bothered him, had driven Mom crazy. In a sudden flash of understanding, I recognized how she must have felt. I just had to be patient and Dad would seek me out.

Shutting down the computer, I turned my mind to more cheerful issues and Dreamcatcher.

* * * *

The next morning dawned with that wreathing mist I had come to expect here in the high hills. The hens were taken care of in record time. Skipping breakfast, I threw a saddle on Bassy, climbed aboard and headed off down the old lane at a lumbering trot, the Shire's huge hooves splattering showers of earth and tiny stones with every pounding step. I didn't have Gyp with me today. Connor was rounding up the sheep and needed the dog. There were no trap marks either, I noticed, viewing the unsullied road ahead.

We had entered the shadowy stretch of woodland when Bassy balked violently and pulled to a startled stop.

"Steady, boy!" I said. "What is it?"

Shires are a breed not known for freaking out and, soothing him with a pat, I threw a puzzled glance around. Everything seemed normal, but right on the edge of my vision I caught a flicker of movement and a shadow slipped between the trees, vanishing into the deeper shadows beyond. It had gotten very still and quiet. There was no birdsong, no rustling of small creatures in the undergrowth, no movement of leaves… just this eerie skin-prickling calm that made me want to hold my breath.

Bassy uttered an uneasy little snort. Anxious to be gone, I gathered up my reins and sent him plunging forwards in a battering trot that put a gratifying distance between us and the freaky woods and brought us at last to the normality of the road.

Alerted by the clop of hooves, Lucy stuck her head out of the cottage window and shouted hello. "What a darling horse," she cried. "He's enormous! Is he easy-going?"

"Very," I said, pulling up. "Bassy's bombproof. It would take an earthquake to spook him." Or an elusive shape in the mossy remnants of an ancient forest, I thought. A cold shiver went down my spine.

Lucy reached out and stroked Bassy's nose. "Cute."

"You can ride him if you want. I'll walk at his head. You'll be fine."

"Maybe some other time, Tessa. It isn't that I don't like horses. I do, very much. But I had a bad experience with my pony when I was little and it scared me permanently." She gave her mouth a rueful quirk. "Silly me! You go along to the stables. Nick's there."

Dismounting, I led Bassy around to the stable yard where Nick pointed us toward an empty stall. Fresh straw covered the floor and there was hay in the rack, which Bassy investigated as I untacked. Finding it to his liking, he settled down to munch.

"Doesn't take much to make him happy," observed Nick from the doorway. "Are you ready for Sunny?"

"Dreamcatcher," I reminded him.

"Sorry. Forgot. Want me to saddle him for you?"

"No, it's all right, thanks. I'll groom him first. "

Nick grabbed a box of grooming equipment, along with Dreamcatcher's simple snaffle bridle and deep all-purpose saddle. "I'll leave you to it, then. The ring is on the other side of the cottage. It's completely enclosed so you'll be safe enough. You might want to walk him around a little before trying anything dramatic."

"Like flying changes, you mean?"

Nick grinned. "He wouldn't know a flying change from a halt."

"Wouldn't he?" I said sweetly. "Then we'll have to teach him."

"That's some challenge. Tweed and Holly are both in their stalls so they won't be a distraction. I'll be around if you want me. Good luck."

Feeling a throb of anticipation, I entered the stable and walked between the rows of stalls to the end stall where Dreamcatcher waited.

"Hello, boy." My voice echoed in the emptiness. "It's me. Remember? Good horse. What a handsome boy."

He wasn't. In the light of the new day he looked uglier than ever and my spirits fell a little. His strange-colored coat, a peculiar mixture of chestnut and brown mottled with gray, lacked the gloss of condition brought about by hard grooming. His mane hung in tatters on either side of his neck, and there was a sore place on his tail where he had rubbed. Making a mental note to ask Nick about worming, I looked at the roan's feet. He was not shod, but the hooves had been recently trimmed and were small and neat and hard as blocks of wood – good hooves.

Offering a Polo mint from my pocket, I watched him crunch it cautiously and spent a while talking to him and letting him get to know me. Then, tying him to the metal ring in the wall, I took a hard-bristled dandy brush from the box and started grooming. Dreamcatcher seemed to like the attention and leaned into my hands, squirming with every movement of the brush, enjoying it. If he'd been a cat he would have purred. I worked until the stable stains and straw were gone and his coat took on some semblance of a gleam. It was satin-like, I saw with surprise. Swapping brushes, I dealt with his tail and straggly mane, removing the longer hairs to even it out.

"There. What a good-looking boy. Now your hooves."

Dreamcatcher submitted readily to having his feet picked out, lifting each one as I asked him, and not snatching them back as some horses do. Some groundwork had been done here, and I hoped the same could be said when I was mounted.

"Now for the tack."

He accepted the snaffle bit with no fuss, raking on it thoughtfully as I did up the throatlash and adjusted the bridle. His deep-set eyes, full of wary intelligence, were watchful as I reached for the saddle and slid it on, gently buckling the girth.

"Okay, let's go."

And without wasting any more time I led him out into the yard and mounted.

I suppose, with Nick's doubts planted in my mind, I was expecting trouble. In reality, there was none. Dreamcatcher turned out to be a very raw youngster, biddable enough but unschooled and unsure of what was required of him. His balance was completely wrong. First he'd lean on the forehead and then throw all his weight behind. He couldn't halt cleanly, and he occasionally led with the correct leg more by luck than design. And yet interspersed through all this were flashes of utter brilliance that made my heart sing. He was a horse eager and willing to learn; the kind that serious riders like best.

After about an hour I put him back in the stable and untacked and rubbed him down, even though he was barely warm.

"So what do you think?"

Nick appeared at the door to the stallion stall, his amused

26

face poking between the strong iron bars that would have kept in a man-eating monster if need be. And this was no monster. This was a horse that had a lot going for him.

"He's terrific," I said.

"Try telling my sister that. She won't come near him. He's made it quite clear what he thinks of her, and me too."

"Maybe he isn't used to male riders. He could sense Lucy's nervousness and that put him on edge. You never know what happened for him to end up at the auction. He's no fool. He could have been badly handled, or anything else."

"Go on. You're making excuses for him. You're infatuated."

"I know. He's so clever and quick, and he just needs work."

"Do you want to school him for me? You could have free rein to do as you please. I watched you riding from the yard. You're good."

"Thanks," I said, heart leaping. "Do you mean it?"

"About riding him? Of course. It'll be great to have someone to go out on trail rides with. It gets boring on your own. You can get up on one of the other horses, if you want."

"I'd love to. Nick, could we start by moving Dreamcatcher out of here? He looks like he's in prison behind these bars. Couldn't he go in one of the stalls?"

"I guess so. We put him in here after he misbehaved. I didn't want Holly and Tweed picking up any bad habits." He glanced at his watch. "I came to tell you Lucy's getting lunch. She said to come over when you're ready. Do you want to move this guy first?"

"Yes, please. Then he can see what's going on around him."

Nick left to attend to the stall. Running a cloth over Dreamcatcher's saddle and bridle, I recalled something odd that had happened out in the ring. The high-railed, soft-floored open schooling ring backed onto a field with show jumps, homemade but good, and then the paddocks. Flanking the ring was the gable end of the smithy's shop. In the bright sunlight the damp-infested old stonework had looked more dismal than ever, which made me shudder involuntarily. And yet try as I might, I could not drag my gaze away. It was as if I were being drawn there against my will.

Sensing my distraction, Dreamcatcher had begun to lag and I quickly pulled myself together. He had broken into a stunningly controlled canter that was like flying and drove all thoughts of creepy old forges from my head.

Now, I couldn't get the incident out of my mind, and when I went inside to mouth-watering homemade soup and crusty bread still warm from the oven, I mentioned what had happened.

"It was freaky. I remember Dad once taking me to see a ruined abbey. I had the same feeling then. Something bad had happened there."

Lucy looked up, soupspoon halfway to her mouth. "What do you mean, bad?"

"I can't remember. It was too long ago. But I've never forgotten the sensation I had."

"Oh, get a grip," Nick said disparagingly. "I school the horses there all the time and I've never noticed anything. It's your imagination getting the better of you. I was thinking of giving Tweed some roadwork afterwards. Want to come on Holly?"

"Sure, sounds great," I said, and the awkward moment was averted. Lucy kept on eating her soup, but she was quiet for the rest of the meal. Nick made up for it, talking nonstop about the upcoming one-day event.

"It's a great venue. You must come and watch, Tessa. I need to put in more work on my show jumping. It's hard to strike a balance between making the horses confident over fences and getting bored. I'll always have problems with Holly and the combinations. She's such a leggy creature, and takes such long loping strides. It's a tossup between going for a clear round and risking time penalties, or going all-out for speed."

"I'd play it safe and do the first. What about the dressage?"

"Oh, we're getting there. It's a fairly basic test. I'll print you out a copy if you want."

"Yes, please. I could teach it to Dreamcatcher."

"You can always try." Nick looked dubious. "He rode well for you this morning, I must say. In fact, great."

After lunch I got up on Sea Holly. She was a wonderful ride with nice smooth paces and a mile-eating stride that was great for picking up time between cross-country fences but, as Nick had said, a little iffy when it came to the tight corners and closely-placed combination obstacles so beloved by designers of show jumping courses. When Nick saw that despite my apparent lack of muscle I could manage her, we went out on a trail ride.

Bassy was dozing in his stall as we clattered out of the yard, and didn't twitch a whisker at being left behind. The same couldn't be said for Dreamcatcher. Now that he was moved into the next stall, he kicked up a big fuss, flinging his head over the door, shrieking, and delivering the woodwork some ramming blows with a fore hoof that echoed like gunshots along the road.

"Fool!" Nick muttered, glancing back over his shoulder. "I hope he doesn't jump out. Heaven help my sister if he does."

"She'd cope. She'd have to."

"Do you think so? We need to get some big gates on the yard. I wanted to make a separate driveway right around the back of the stables that comes out at the smithy. It would have saved some awkward maneuvering for the horse trailer and made the yard more secure for the horses. The guys who did the renovations weren't eager to do it, though."

"Why not?"

"They were local guys. They get funny notions. We had a hard enough job finding a builder who'd do the renovations as it was."

"But why?"

"Oh, reasons," Nick said, riding on, his gaze fixed between Tweed's large ears.

A stream of cars came up behind us and we dropped into single file to let them pass. Once the road was clear again I nudged Holly back alongside the chestnut.

"These two are good in traffic, aren't they? I wonder what Dreamcatcher's like."

"He's not bad at all. I took him for a ride the day he ditched me, thinking it might get the tickle out of his feet."

"And did it?"

Nick's mouth twisted wryly. "No."

"Oh dear," I said on a quiver of laughter. "He hasn't taken to you, has he?"

We were approaching Rydale now. Ahead, the main street bustled with traffic and shoppers, and when Nick didn't answer I thought nothing of it. It took a moment or two to realize what a mixed reception we were getting. People who were strangers to the district – vacationers, canoeists and so on – stopped to watch us trot by. The rest ignored us. It was as if the residents of Rydale didn't want to know the boy from the forge with the merry blue eyes and friendly slanting grin.

31

Head up, his face impassive, Nick trotted on along the street, the big horse covering the distance rapidly. I followed in silence and was glad to reach the curved stone bridge with the coffee shop at its foot, which signified the end of the village. We clopped over the bridge and came to open country.

Once clear of Rydale, Nick perked up and began to point out places of interest. We saw the canoeing center where a team of paddlers braved the rapids in their flimsy craft. Further on was a series of caves that tunneled deep into the hillside. And then, best of all, there was a racing stable. Here a string of horses came pounding unexpectedly along the trail on the other side of the hedge, setting our mounts frolicking.

"Whoa!" Nick shouted, holding in a prancing Tweed whose oversized ears flopped hilariously with every movement. "You okay, Tessa?"

Holly was dancing on the spot. "Just about," I gasped, weak with laughter. "It's Tweed! He looks so funny. He's too big to act like a naughty pony!"

"Maybe that's what he thinks he is!" Nick said.

"Could be." The racehorses had gone careering off and were now no more than smudges of color in the distance. "I never can decide which I like best. I see a bunch of Thoroughbreds like those and think there's nothing better. Last spring I went to look at a Shetland stud and felt exactly the same."

"That's a big difference! But I know what you mean. You like the whole scene equally. My grandmother would have said it's the best way to be. She was a wise old woman."

"Was she? Do you miss her?"

"Yes, a lot. She was a rock. She encouraged us to follow

32

our own talents and strengths. It was Grandma who made sure Lucy went to Art College and put money aside for me to take equestrian training when I leave school." Nick paused, looking across at me, his eyes very blue under the black peak of his riding hat. "What about you, Tessa? Do you have any ideas about a career? What about the jazz scene? You've got quite an act to follow, with your mom."

"It isn't a consideration. I can't sing a note in tune. I play the piano, but only for my own amusement. I'd like to do something with horses, but don't have a clue what."

"Maybe veterinary work? You've got what it takes. You could specialize."

"Maybe, but I'm not really sure."

"Oh well, you've got time to make up your mind. Let's trot, okay?"

All too soon the newly tiled roof of the Old Forge came into view and we were clopping into the stable yard, having ridden in a large circle. Dreamcatcher – still in his stall – started squealing and bashing the door again, bringing a shout of reproof from Nick. We turned the horses out in the big field behind the paddocks, after which I returned to the roan and groomed him until Nick said I'd wear out the brush!

Over the distant forest, the sun was dipping in smudges of crimson and gold. The swallows that nested under the eaves of the stables began their evening flight, feeding on the gnats that rose in pestering swarms. After making arrangements to ride again tomorrow, I fetched Bassy and hauled myself stiffly onto his back. It had been a long day. I wanted to get back and wallow in a warm bath before supper.

I should have known better, for nothing here was turning out that simple. I was unprepared for the icy breath of wind that brushed my warm cheeks as we thudded up the sunken lane, Bassy's gait slow and ponderous after Sea Holly's light step and Dreamcatcher's raciness. Entering the woods, we plunged into such an uncanny dimness that my hands tightened in alarm on the reins. Slightly ahead, on the overgrown path veined with the roots of trees, a figure stood, causing me to pull up sharply, Bassy snorting his indignation.

That was my first meeting with Annie Shone.

CHAPTER THREE

Dressed in rusty colors that blended amazingly with her surroundings, she must have been gathering wild plants, for a wicker basket on the side of the path was full to the brim. She had wildly curling black hair swept back in an untidy knot at the nape of her neck and a strong face that was freckled and burnished by the weather.

"Hello," she greeted, bright dark eyes taking me in. "You must be the girl from the farm. I'm Annie Shone."

Smiling engagingly, she planted herself firmly on the path in front of me.

"Hi," I said, hoping she wouldn't hold me up for long. There was no obvious sign of a vehicle – no farm truck or bicycle – and it crossed my mind to wonder how she had gotten here. We were quite far from any houses for a person to be roaming the woods on foot.

"It's been a long walk, but then I'm used to it," she chirped, almost as if she had read my thoughts. "And I needed the nettles."

It got odder. "What?"

"Nettles," she repeated, indicating her basket. "There's none better than these in Black Woods."

The small thicket of scattered trees and bushes seemed somehow vaster and denser. Darker. A real forest, and not the airy straggle of greenery I knew.

"Oh, right," I said, struggling to overcome the unease that was stealing over me. More than anything I wanted to get away, but she had other ideas. Standing firmly in the path, she nodded toward Bassy, who had made the most of the halt and was dozing.

"Nice horse you're riding. He's what my man would have called an honest sort. He'll be good between the shafts."

"Yes, he is. My stepbrother does logging with the horses. I go with him to the forest sometimes."

"That's heavy work for a girl," she said kindly. "Still, we've got to help each other out, haven't we." She peered closer at Bassy. "Prone to eye trouble, is he? You need chickweed for that."

"Oh?" First nettles, now chickweed. Interested despite myself, I said, "It sounds like you make your own herbal medicines. That's cool! We buy ours from the health food store."

"I've always brewed my own!" sniffed Annie, who clearly didn't think much of the manufactured product. "It was my mother who taught me. She was a great one for healing, animals in particular. You need to be careful with them, especially horses. They can't take strong doses like us." She picked up her basket. "Well, mustn't keep you any longer, Tessa. I'll see you again, no doubt."

She went on her way, long skirt slapping around her slim form, and her feet in sturdy boots making light work of the soggy path. Relieved, I gave Bassy's sides a nudge to wake him up and continued in the opposite direction. At the next bend I risked a glance over my shoulder. There was no sign of Annie, and the woods had lightened around me, though that could have been due to the sun setting in golden shafts between the branches of oak and quivering mountain ash.

"Come on, Bassy. Home!"

He didn't need to be told twice. Sensing his stable and the feed that waited, he mustered up a stamping trot that quickly brought us to the farm.

* * * *

Over supper, I asked Connor about the person in the woods.

"There are a number of isolated hamlets up in the hills. She must be from one of those," Connor said indifferently.

"She said the thicket of trees on the lane was called Black Woods."

"That's likely. Every hill, field and wood has a name. It'll be on an early ordnance survey map of the region, if you're interested. There's one in the dresser. What else did she say?"

"She went on about Bassy's eyes. I checked when I got back, but he seems okay."

"He wasn't last winter," Connor said. "He had conjunctivitis. The vet prescribed a course of antibiotics but it didn't do any good. The problem would clear up and then come back again. It cost me a small fortune, too."

"She said chickweed was the best cure."

"Is that right? The old remedies are making a comeback. There was a talk on the radio by one of those holistic practitioners. Very interesting, up to a point." Connor shoveled more potatoes onto his plate. "How did Bassy behave for you?"

"Fine, thanks. Lucy said he was cute."

Snorting a laugh, Connor remarked that cute wasn't a word he'd have used for half a ton of Shire. He went on to ask about Dreamcatcher and I launched into a glowing epistle that lasted to the end of the meal.

It was only afterwards, drifting off to sleep in bed, that I remembered with a jolt that the woman had called me by my name. I hadn't introduced myself, so how had she known? It was also strange that she had known where I lived. Pondering, I chalked it up to the local grapevine, or as Eddie refers to it, the bush telegraph, and on that comforting note I fell asleep. I dreamed of the horse again, only this time he had taken shape as an odd-colored roan that was carrying me to victory at one of those hair-raising competitions I would never in real life have had the nerve to enter.

* * * *

I couldn't let the matter of Annie Shone drop, and the next morning I looked at the land map Connor had mentioned. Sure enough, marked on the thick parchment that was splitting at the folds was Black Woods. The map was dated around the turn of the last century, when land was gradually being registered, and the woods were much bigger. Cross Hill Farm was there, a well-to-do property. Oddly, the Old Forge was not named. All it showed was a tiny box to indicate a dwelling. I wondered how long the smithy had been out of use and where people had gone to get their farm implements repaired and horses shod. Nick had said he used the traveling farrier now.

Putting the map away, I went to saddle Bassy. Today the ride was uneventful, the lane free of tracks, and Black Woods no more than an unkempt straggle of trees and bushy undergrowth, a haunt of birds and scampering rabbits. It seemed so ordinary that yesterday's experience was relegated to the realms of imagination. Bassy stepped out happily, eager to return to his comfy new stall and the hay that awaited.

"Hi," called Lucy from the courtyard behind the cottage, where she was watering the plants. "I'll be with you in a moment. I'm dying for a cup of coffee. Would you mind making some, Tessa?"

Nick was in the ring, schooling Sea Holly in careful circles. He looked absorbed, so without interrupting I settled Bassy in his stall and went in to make coffee. As I took down some mugs from the cupboard I noticed, draped on the back of a chair, one of Lucy's shawls in vivid colors. On impulse I picked it up, arranging it over my shoulders the way Mom did. At that moment Lucy came in. She stopped in the doorway, studying the effect, and then shook her head.

"It's not you, Tessa. It's too bright."

"Mom would look fantastic in it. Nothing looks right on me."

"Oh, I wouldn't say that. You've got your own style."

I must have looked dubious, for she went on, "You need a more subtle look to show off that gorgeous skin and hair. Trendy, yet countrified. Just a minute."

She went running up the stairs and came back with a really classy corduroy shirt in a soft mink-brown color, which she insisted I try on. When I did, she nodded approvingly. "Yes, I thought so. That shade does nothing for me at all, but it looks terrific on you. Take it, go on."

"Are you sure?" I asked, fingering the lovely smooth fabric.

"Of course. You'll need something to wear with it. Pants, or maybe a skirt and top. Something understated. We could go into town one day and hit the shops. It'll be fun. We're sure to find the very thing."

"Great," I said, running my fingers through my shorn locks. "What about this? Do you think it would suit me if I grew it out, like yours? Long hair is so versatile."

"True, but no, I wouldn't. That way is totally you. It's a good cut."

"Mom's stylist did it for me. Mom's got beautiful hair," I said.

"So do you. One doesn't have to be blonde and glamorous to be attractive. It's like I said. You have to cultivate your own look. Work at it." She smiled. "Come on, let's have a drink, and then you can go and saddle up. Nick said something about you riding Dreamcatcher. You will be careful?"

"Oh, don't worry. I might not have much fashion sense but I do know how to look after myself." I took off the shirt and put it carefully over the chair. "Thank you for that."

"My pleasure," Lucy said simply.

Shortly afterwards I went back out again into the sunshine. Dreamcatcher was in one of the paddocks and came pounding toward me at my call, tossing his head and slamming on his brakes just as he reached the gate.

"Show off! Here's your mint."

He took the treat delicately, rolling it around in his mouth before crunching it – and nosing around for more.

"Afterwards, if you behave," I told him. Clipping on the lead rope, I led him to his stall. Nick had finished working Holly and was putting a saddle on Tweed.

"I thought about going up to the cliffs," he called. "It's a long ride. Are you game?"

"I am if Dreamcatcher is," I said.

Dreamcatcher was full of himself and fidgeted as I mounted, sidestepping and tossing his head with a noisy rattle of bit rings. "Stand," I ordered, hopping, one foot in the stirrup. "Be good."

He gave in with a good-natured suddenness and I swung up into the saddle, urging him to the gate where Nick waited on Rough Tweed. The big liver chestnut stood resigned, regarding the younger horse's antics with mild astonishment down his long aristocratic nose. Beside him, Dreamcatcher looked like a mere pony, and a not a very attractive one at that. It didn't bother me. He had something, a vital ingredient that told me he was a winner.

"Do you think a person should choose a horse for its looks?" I said as we set off, Dreamcatcher dancing a little, Rough Tweed striding out sensibly.

"No," Nick replied. "I'd never have bought Dream-catcher if that was the case. Though I have to admit, I fell for Sea Holly's appearance. She's got such glamour. I think it's best to choose the horse that's right for you."

"My riding instructor says there are people who buy really good horses and never get anywhere with them. He says you have to be able to ride a good horse."

"He's right." Nick threw Dreamcatcher an appraising glance. "He does well with you. It's amazing what a difference it makes now that he's properly on the bit. He looks like a different horse. He could have some Arab blood in him. That would account for his toughness and light movement. I think that's what attracted me to him at the sale. There was a moment when he was being paraded around the sale ring and he looked really good. Arabian, you know."

"Yes. It would account for his intelligence as well."

"Craftiness, my sister calls it. Wait till you start jumping him. I bet he'll have tremendous spring."

"It'll be a long time before he's ready for that."

"I don't see why. When we get back I'll rig up a cavalletti for you." This was a row of poles on the ground. "It won't do any harm to trot him over it."

"All right," I said, "Great."

We had taken the road away from the village and were now

41

climbing steadily between rugged stretches of open heath. Dreamcatcher, it turned out, had a disconcerting spooking habit that caught me by surprise when a breeze ruffled some tall grass with a dry rustling sound, and later when a pheasant burst out of a thicket and shot across our path.

"Steady!" I said, sitting tight, trying to keep my balance as he frolicked manically on the spot. As before, he stopped as quickly as he had begun and walked on, looking bemused.

Nick laughed. "He's athletic, isn't he? Probably more so than either Tweed or Holly."

Yes, he was a quick, clever horse that would be great in the jumping ring, fast and agile across country and yet balanced and responsive in the dressage arena. In other words, he was the perfect event animal for Nick. I wished – how I *wished* – things were different and Dreamcatcher could be mine.

"I printed out that dressage test you wanted," said Nick. "I don't know about you, but my biggest problem is remembering the sequence of those things. I have to chant it like a mantra to get it to sink in. I was reciting this one in the supermarket the other day and got some very strange looks."

"Oh, stop!" I cracked up, laughing, "I don't believe you!"

"Don't you? Did anyone ever tell you what an infectious laugh you have?"

His look was warm and I blushed. "Let's trot, and see if your fellow can keep up with Tweed," Nick said.

We quickened our pace. It was great to be riding out together under the blue summer sky, the mountain birds winging overhead, sheep dotted across the rolling green landscape like drifts of snow, the air pure and grass-scented. My troubles receded magically. I didn't mind so much about Mom and Eddie any more, and decided I

wouldn't dwell on Dad and disappointments any more. Live for the moment, he used to say. Today I was doing just that.

When we got back I went straight into the ring while Nick grabbed some training poles from the corner of the jumping paddock. Dreamcatcher was a quick learner. Once he understood what was expected of him he trotted and cantered over them without any trouble.

"Great!" shouted Nick from the rails. "Try the colored ones. See what he does."

This was a different matter, and Dreamcatcher freaked! Plain natural fences were acceptable, it seemed, but a dazzle of white poles striped with black and yellow was an enemy to be avoided, provoking such ferocious snorts and hilariously popping eyes that Nick nearly fell off the fence laughing.

"He's like a dragon!" Nick spluttered. "You should see him! What a comedian!"

"Well, don't just sit there!" I said helplessly, torn between mirth and the wish to get the horse over the poles. "Can't you do something?"

Red-faced and grinning, Nick came to assist. Between us, we eventually persuaded Dreamcatcher to hop over the dreaded horror on the ground. Once he would take them without balking, I unsaddled and turned him out on the small paddock next to Holly and Tweed. He went straight to a muddy corner and rolled, after which he stood up, shook himself thoroughly and got down to the serious business of grazing.

Leaving him to it, I mucked out the stall and cleaned the tack. Then, gathering up the shirt from Lucy, I saddled Bassy and headed home. Hopeful of seeing Annie to ask more about the chickweed remedy, I was disappointed to find Black

44

Woods deserted. The trees rustled their leaves guilelessly; the only sign of life a squirrel cavorting in the branches.

At Cross Hill I put Bassy in his field, a long meadow overlooking the dark line of forest. He didn't roll as Dreamcatcher had, but stood by the gate, watching for his stablemate to come home. He looked lonely, so I stayed with him for a while, spoiling him with a crust of bread from the kitchen.

There was still no sign of Connor, so to pass the time I went to the tack room and started cleaning the spare harness. Connor was very particular about the tack. He checked it regularly for wear and frayed stitching and made sure to alternate the sets, so that each received the same amount of use. When I got to polishing the head brass pieces, I paused. In the cupboard where the cleaning gear was kept was a battered wooden box of assorted bits and buckles. Among them were some brass pieces other than plain flashes like these.

Taking down the box, I made my selection; a stunning heraldic piece featuring trefoils and crests and another showing mythical beasts, both far more decorative than the existing ones. Buffing them until they were bright and sparkling, I buckled them onto the browbands, hung the bridles on their pegs and thought no more of it.

Until a couple of mornings later.

Connor was running late. He was working in a particularly overgrown area of the forest and needed both horses. Just as he was going to get them, a man called about having some trees felled and held Connor up haggling over the price. Settled at last, Connor hurried out. Moments later there was a shout.

"TESSA? WHAT'S ALL THIS?"

It sounded urgent. I stopped what I was doing, tore across to the stables and came upon Connor ripping the replacement brass pieces off the driving bridles. He looked up as I entered, his face clouded with annoyance and something else that I couldn't put a name to.

"Who told you to swap these brass pieces?" he snapped.

"Nobody. I thought those would be a nice change."

"That's not the point. You shouldn't have done it, Tessa. Where are the flashes?"

"In the tack room," I said. "Why? Connor, what's wrong?"

"Just get them, please."

I did as he asked and watched in bewilderment as he grimly buckled them back onto the brow bands. Ready to go at last, he clambered onto the cart and took up the reins. "I'll leave Gyp with you today. Make sure you take him with you when you go out."

"Okay," I said.

Connor clicked his tongue to the horses and sent the cart rumbling out of the yard. Chastened, and more than a little put out, I returned to the house.

In the glass-fronted bookcase in the front room was a book on brass horse hardware and this is where I headed, running my finger down the list of the various types until I came to those used as headpieces.

"Flash," I read aloud. "A flat circular plate said to thwart evil. Wow!"

CHAPTER FOUR

My head reeled as I called Gyp and we set off for the Old Forge, crossing the farmyard, skirting the corner of the outbuildings, and making for the stone steps that led onto the lane. It was a dull morning, gnats dancing in the air, the sun lost behind thick banks of cloud. Reaching the steps, I stopped short.

The tracks were here again. There was something weird about those tracks and I hesitated, biting my lip, torn between carrying on and taking the longer route via the road. At my heels, Gyp gave a troubled little whine. I thought of Dreamcatcher. Nick had promised to bring him in. He'd be waiting and impatient.

"Come, Gyp. Let's go."

He took the steps in a bound and I followed, clambering down with slightly less enthusiasm. We headed off down the lane, my feet in leather riding boots sloshing on the wet ground, with Gyp padding silently beside me. So clear were the tracks that at every bend I expected to see what had made them. It didn't happen. We passed through Black Woods and out again. I heard Gyp panting, his tongue lolling, and realized I had unwittingly quickened my step.

Just as before, the tracks led all the way down to the road. Sticky from the heat and breathless, we arrived at the cottage. Lucy was in the den, swathed from head to foot in a bulky sackcloth apron, preparing some fiber for dyeing. Simmering pungently on a portable stove was a large cauldron of dye-immersed wool.

"Hello, you two," Lucy said. "You look hot. Been running?"

"It's this weather. Do you think we're in for a storm?"

"Could be. We get them unexpectedly here in the hills. They're over quickly, though."

Gyp made a dive for the water bowl by the door and lapped thirstily. Mopping my damp face with the back of my hand, I sank onto a stool and was about to blurt out what had happened with the brass horse hardware and the reappearance of the strange tracks, when I thought again. Lucy might think I was neurotic. Besides, Connor had every right to dress up his harness with flashes if that's what he wanted. And wasn't everyone a little bit superstitious at heart? As for the tracks – well, there had to be a reason for them.

What I did say was, "Lucy, do you believe in bad luck?"

She looked up quickly as if in alarm, but collected herself immediately. "Like never walking under ladders and not stepping on cracks in the pavement? Is that what you mean?"

"In a way. There's a girl at school who does those things deliberately. She thinks if you don't believe in it then nothing can happen."

"She could be right." Shrugging and dismissive, she gave her dye pot a jab with the wooden spoon. "Are you riding this morning? You could be in for a good soaking."

"I'd better get a move on, then."

Out in the yard, Nick was waiting with horses saddled. The first large drops of rain began as we set off into the darkening morning. Long before we reached the village it became a deluge, causing Holly to flatten her ears and tuck in her tail miserably. Nick gave her shoulder an encouraging slap.

"Poor Holly. She hates the rain. Your fellow doesn't seem to be bothered."

48

Dreamcatcher jogged happily through the downpour, sidestepping the puddles – another indication of his Arabian forebears, since Arabs notoriously dislike getting their hooves wet – and aiming an occasional little nip at the mare as we went.

"He's got it in for Holly for some reason," Nick observed. "I can't imagine why. She's the most inoffensive creature." A farm truck swept by, showering us with muddy spray and causing a grumble of annoyance from Nick. "You're quiet, Tessa. Is anything wrong? Don't tell me you're allergic to rain?"

"Not that I know of," I said soberly.

The day's start had left its mark. I couldn't get Connor, and the way he had shouted at me, out of my mind. The weather didn't help either – though one good thing would come of the rain. Those bewildering prints that nobody would acknowledge would be completely washed away.

As Lucy had predicted, the storm was soon over. The sun appeared, bright and warm, and by the time we got back to the house we were dry again.

"No way am I eating in the house today," said Nick. "Not while my sister's in dye-pot mode. Ugh, the stink!"

I looked up from running a currycomb over Dreamcatcher. "Let's all eat at the Tavern." This was the popular coffee house by the river. "My treat. Oh, come on!"

Nick hesitated, but only briefly. "Okay, thanks. I'll go ask Lucy, okay?"

"Sure, it'll be a nice change for her."

I should have known better because, just like the last time, as we entered the village we were met with frosty faces. At the coffee shop the service was excellent, the food great, but even here our presence seemed barely tolerated.

49

It was not my imagination. Something here was badly wrong. I was glad to get back to Dreamcatcher and the schooling routine I had worked out for him.

He was great for me that afternoon. I had memorized the dressage test and began teaching the transitions. None of it was beyond Dreamcatcher's abilities. A few more sessions and he would have the test down perfectly.

We finished with the colored poles and this time he dropped his nose and trotted over them, still cautious but obedient to my commands.

"I'll fix up a low jump tomorrow," Nick said. "He'll fly over it."

I was starting to feel more cheerful. Lucy improved my spirits further by handing over several more unwanted items of clothing.

"Those tops are exactly you," she said. "You're so lovely and willowy. Is your mother tall?"

"No." Holding a sweater in front of me, I studied the effect in the mirror. "Mom's just right. It doesn't matter what she wears because she always looks great. You must have seen her on TV."

"Yes, but the camera doesn't always give a true picture."

"I take after my dad," I said. "The same floppy hair and boring hazel eyes. I must remind her of him. I wonder if it bothers her."

"You looking like your father, you mean?" Lucy was incredulous. "Surely not. She's your mom. She loves you. You get along with Eddie Boyd, don't you?"

"Oh, yes. Everyone likes Eddie. He's great. I miss Dad, though. I used to tag along with him on field trips. He's a geologist. He likes horses too."

"A big plus." Lucy smiled, sympathy in her eyes.

"Oh well, let's find a bag for these things. It's a good thing you're on foot today, Tessa. It'll be easier to carry them."

As I had supposed, on the homeward journey the tracks on the lane had vanished, but whether it was due to the rain or a more cunning source I had no way of knowing.

Connor was already home. A very contrite Connor. He pointed to a giant bar of milk chocolate on the table. "It's a peace offering. I'm sorry about this morning, Tessa."

"That's okay. How was Bassy?"

"Fine. I won't need him for the rest of the week, so consider him yours. Supper's in the oven. I hope you're hungry. It's a roast."

Still full after eating out, I struggled to do justice to Connor's effort at making matters right between us. It had been a mess of a day and it did not help matters when Mom called, bursting with talk about the gigs, bringing home to me just how far removed her world was from mine.

"We're having such a marvelous time, darling. There's never a dull moment. How are you doing at Cross Hill? Not too bored?"

"Not at all." I took a breath and mentioned Dreamcatcher. "Mom, he's a star. He actually wants to learn. It's amazing when a horse is like that."

"Oh, really?"

There it was, the immediate withdrawal. Mom would never understand my obsession with horses. To her they were big, boisterous creatures that made me smell like a stable and drip hayseeds on the carpets. Even Eddie had not been able to convince her otherwise.

"Do you have him with you at Cross Hill?" Mom enquired.

51

"No, he belongs to Nick Meredith in the village. Nick's sister is Lucy Meredith." I waited for the impact to strike. It was there in an instant.

"*The* Lucy Meredith? Oh, well! What is she like?"

"Terrific. She's given me some clothes she didn't want."

"Has she? I'm impressed! I could never get you interested in dressing up. Have you seen her latest line?" This was more Mom's scene, and for a while we chatted about Lucy and the pending business. "Eddie wants a word," Mom said at last. "He's dying to know what you think of Cross Hill."

"Tessa? Hi," boomed Eddie's voice before I could catch my breath. "How're things?"

"Fine, thanks," I said. "It's great here for riding."

"There's plenty of open country, isn't there? Have you come across the tracks yet?"

"What?" My throat went suddenly dry.

"Just some local yarn. These horse and buggy tracks are supposed to appear on that old cattle driver's route behind the farm. I never saw them myself, and I don't think Connor has either. I don't know, to be honest. It isn't a thing we ever talked about. Tessa, you still there?"

"Yes," I answered, faintly.

"The story goes that the horse was a killer and went around terrorizing the neighborhood... Hang on a minute, your mother's trying to talk. You've found something decent to ride? Oh, great. Dreamcatcher, eh? That's a name and a half!"

"Dreamcatcher's a horse and a half," I said. This was much safer ground, and for a while we talked real flesh-and-blood horses rather than the ghostly variety. Eddie was enthusing about a part-bred Arab he'd once had and how great it was, when there was a swift burst of background noise and I guessed the members of the band had turned up from wherever they had been. Sure enough, the conversation was cut short and I was handed back to Mom. We said goodbye and hung up.

My hand was shaking as I replaced the receiver. Phantom prints. That was no good. Whatever it took, I had to find out more.

****

"I'm sorry, I can't tell you."

The woman behind the counter of the general store pressed her lips together in a stubborn line. I tried again.

"But I don't understand. Lucy and Nick Meredith are really great. Lucy's a rising name on the fashion scene. A shop would bring income to the village. That can't be a bad thing."

Silence. Giving up, I bought some chocolate (badly needed), a pack of licorice that Connor had admitted a weakness for, and some mints for the horses, and went out again into the soft morning air.

Nibbling the chocolate, I wandered down the street and came to a pharmacy, which had postcards of paintings depicting local scenes displayed on a board by the door. Deciding to send some to family and friends, I made a selection and went inside to pay. The store had a wide range of alternative medicines, including a glass cabinet of essential oils, some very rare and expensive. I paused to look at them.

"There's a leaflet," said the girl at the cash register helpfully. "It's free."

I picked one off the pile, shoving it in my pocket, then went over to the register. As the girl handed me my change, she looked me over closely.

53

"You're from the farm, aren't you? Connor's place."

"That's right. I ride the horses at the Old Forge."

"Yes, I've seen you go past with the boy. She doesn't ride. The sister."

"Lucy? No. She used to, but she lost her nerve. One of the horses in the stable took a bite out of her. That hasn't helped."

"No, it wouldn't. I remember them coming in here to ask the pharmacist to check the injury. It hadn't broken the skin but it was a nasty bruise." The girl frowned. "Well, what can you expect."

I stared at her. "Excuse me?"

"He was a young horse, wasn't he? New to the place. He'd have picked up the vibes."

"I don't understand. What vibes?"

The girl shook her head. "That'd be telling and we don't, not around here. All I can say is that the Old Forge is known to have a bad feel about it. You should keep away. I know I would."

"But that's ridiculous!" I burst out. "It's just superstition!"

"Maybe, but what's the sense in taking chances?" the girl said.

Knowing I'd get nothing more from her, I pocketed my purchases and left.

****

Back at the yard, Nick had brought the horses in. We had a routine established now: we'd start with a trail ride, and then Nick jumped Holly and Tweed while I put Dreamcatcher through his track work. Lunch followed, after which the tack cleaning, stable chores and often more work in the saddle took up the afternoon. Today, the words of the girl at the pharmacy haunted me. I kept glancing toward the boarded-up smithy. What lay behind those wooden barriers? Would I ever find out? Finally, desperate to have some light shed on the mystery, I cornered Nick in the tack room. He was putting together a bridle, the pieces displayed tidily on the bench beside him.

"Nick. About the blacksmith's shop. There's something odd there. What is it?"

"Don't ask questions you might not like the answers to," he replied without stopping what he was doing.

"But I need to know," I pressed on. "There's something weird going on here. I'm determined to find out somehow. Why not just come clean, here and now?"

He put down the half-assembled bridle. His face was serious. "Look, Tessa. There are some things around here that are better left unsaid. If it means so much to you, why don't you try Connor?"

"Some good that would do! Connor's as bad as the rest of you. He'll clam up the way you have. When I spoke with Eddie on the phone he mentioned mysterious tracks on the lane. Nick, I've seen those tracks. They come and go. It's freaky. I want to know what it's all about."

"Then you'll have to do your digging elsewhere. Sorry, Tessa. It's a sensitive issue, so let's forget it."

I gazed at him, stubborn, unyielding. Nick grinned encouragingly. "Did I mention I put up a few more cross-country fences on the fields? Thought I'd see how Holly copes with them. Want to come on Tweed?"

"You're changing the subject," I told him accusingly. "But okay. Is that Tweed's bridle you've got there? I'll go and get him ready, okay?"

* * * *

As always, once I was in the saddle all else was put aside.

The land was ideally dotted with thickets, spreading hedges and low stone walls. In addition, Nick had built some natural fences, swinging a pole here, a line of brushwood there, and making use of any fallen tree across the path.

"This is great," I said. "Do you think Dreamcatcher could manage it?"

"We could always try at some point," Nick said obligingly. "Ready? Then let him go."

I set Tweed at the first fence, some low brush that he hopped over without seeming to notice. He was a steady, comfortable ride and galloped powerfully around the obstacles, taking each one in stride. Pulling up by the field gate where there was a clear view of the course, I watched Nick take Holly around the course. His assessment of the mare was perfectly accurate. She needed to be bolder at jumping, but made up for it with a blistering turn of speed between fences.

"She'll get there, in time," Nick said, slapping the mare's neck in praise. "What do you think of Tweed?"

"He's fine. Work on his dressage and he should stand a chance at that event."

"There's less than a month to go. I think I'll give the course another try. Come on, Holly."

Time slipped by and I was late tacking up for home. Dear old Bassy seemed to be plodding more than ever after my day on the powerful warmblood Dreamcatcher, and lumbered along up the trail with Gyp bounding on ahead. The mystery behind those tracks seethed in my mind. How did they vanish so completely, seemingly in the blink of an eye? Who was the rampaging horse that was supposed to have made them? Had he really existed, or was it some tall tale cooked up long ago to frighten children into behaving themselves? Common sense told me that the latter was more likely, and that the tracks had a logical explanation.

We arrived at Black Woods and on impulse I dismounted to search for signs of those elusive prints. I figured that on the open trail the natural drying out process of sun and wind might reasonably account for them being obliterated. Here under the trees, however, where the ground was shaded and damp, some trace must surely remain. Pushing back the bracken and bushes that overhung the path, with Bassy's reins clutched in my free hand, I searched the ground intently and did not notice the woods growing deeper and darker around me. Then, at my side, Gyp growled a warning and a voice said, "Hello, Tessa."

I looked up and there she was – Annie Shone, a shapeless old coat over her long dress. Today it was berries she had in her basket. I wondered what they were for.

"Jam," Annie said in that brain-blowing way she had of reading one's mind. "Are you picking too?"

"No. I was looking for the tracks," I told her.

Annie's face tightened. "Ah. That'll be the horse."

"You've seen it?" I cried with delight. Here was the proof that put an end to the spooky rumor. Eddie had to be wrong. There was no ghost horse, no phantom carriage. What he'd told me was pure fantasy.

"All those who have crossed the stream have seen it," Annie said in the next breath, confusing me further.

"What? Which stream? There are lots along here."

"Not *a* stream. *The* stream."

I heaved a sigh, wishing she wouldn't talk this way. It made her sound deranged and I hoped she wasn't. Eccentric maybe. Out of her mind, no. Her revelation didn't help at

all, and my previous doubts came surging back, laced now with disappointment. She was frowning, her eyes darting, as if unpleasant thoughts chased behind them.

"Annie, what is it?" I whispered. "What's wrong?"

She started to mutter and mumble distractedly and I couldn't quite catch what she said, only the words 'horse' and 'smithy', which made me prick up my ears.

"Which horse?" I pressed. "The one with the trap? Annie, what do you mean?"

Annie didn't answer but continued her wild and incoherent liturgy on whatever it was that troubled her. A sudden explosive sneeze from Bassy put an end to it. Jerked abruptly out of her reverie, Annie watched as he shook his head in irritation and bent to scratch his nose on his knee, bit rings rattling noisily. "Your Bassy must be sensitive to pollen," Annie said, her usual self once more. "That'll be why his eyes bother him at times. Did you pass on my tip about the chickweed?"

"Yes, I did. Connor said he might try it if the problem crops up again." That was when I remembered the holistic leaflet in my pocket, and everything else was driven from my mind. "Annie, do you know anything about aromatherapy?"

"Aroma – what?"

"Therapy. It's the use of precious oils to heal. You must have heard of it."

"I've heard of juice of rosemary and citronella for the sweet itch. Is that what you're thinking of?"

"Sort of," I said. Sweet itch was a summertime horse scourge, especially among susceptible native breeds, causing the ponies to rub their manes and tails until they were raw and bleeding. There were many preparations for it on the market but nothing really cured the condition.

"I think it's to do with the way our bodies react to scents. Like lavender being good for motion sickness. Citronella will detract fleas, won't it? Combined with the rosemary, I guess it will drive off the gnats that cause the itching and help calm the skin irritation at the same time."

"That's right. Worked it out for yourself, didn't you?" Annie looked at me with new respect. "You're a healer in the making, Tessa."

A healer. I caught my breath, seized by a sudden excitement. That was it! The elusive career that I knew had to exist for me. I could be a holistic practitioner like the one Connor had spoken of, except that I would specialize in equines. I'd have my own shop and deal with every aspect of the horse world, from racing yards to pet ponies. The prospect was thrilling. I couldn't keep the smile from my face.

Annie's black eyes were on me, bright and knowing. "Famous, you'll be one day, Tessa. A name on everyone's lips," she said sanguinely.

She sounded so certain, so convincing, that I almost believed her. But reason prevailed. Nobody could predict the future. Maybe she was a little nutty after all, but it was the nicest kind of nuttiness and I grinned affectionately at her.

It was getting late and Bassy shifted his weight restlessly, wanting his field of grass. Gyp had already sneaked off home. Annie said goodbye, hitched her basket over her arm and went walking away into the darkness of the trees. Remounting, I rode on to the farm. Gyp was waiting by the back door, looking repentant at having abandoned us.

"Some guard you are!" I grumbled, sliding down from the saddle. "What got into you? It's those tracks, isn't it? You're as freaked by them as I am." Gyp fixed me with that hard stare that collies have, as if he knew more than I ever would. "I wish you could talk. And what's more, I wish I could solve this mystery."

It seemed impossible.

Standing very still in the sunlit farmyard, conscious of the busy clucking of the hens in the orchard and the mingled smell of sheep and horse and clean mountain air, I looked up at the rolling hills where the old cattle driver's road wound away into the blue distance, and a thought occurred that made me wonder why it hadn't struck before.

Why not follow the road and see where it led? Excitement caught me. Maybe I'd come across the source of those baffling prints. It could bring me to where Annie lived, and then we could discuss the subject of herbal cures more fully, without her having to rush off suddenly the way she did.

I couldn't go on Bassy; he was too slow. Dreamcatcher would get me there quickly – assuming that Nick would let me take the horse out on my own.

Once started, a plan unfolded. Not only would I investigate the old lane, I'd do the same with that crazy shutdown smithy and find out what secrets it held!

Earlier, Lucy had mentioned wanting to see her accountant in the city, a two-hour drive away. Nick had jumped at the chance of going as well, since he needed to visit the equine superstore for blankets and travel boots for the one-day event.

Lucy had asked if I would look after things while they were gone.

No problem, I had said, not thinking how opportune this would be. Now, the idea seemed perfect. Having the place to myself for several hours was ideal. I could sneak a look inside the blacksmith's shop, replace the boards on the door, and nobody would be any the wiser.

My mind made up, I turned Bassy out in his field and went inside to look up the training requirements for holistic equine therapy on the Internet.

CHAPTER FIVE

"I don't see why not," Nick said at my suggestion that Dreamcatcher would benefit from being ridden out alone. "He still freaks out sometimes. Are you sure you'll be okay?"

That earned him the withering look he deserved, and Nick backed off with a grin that made my heart tug. I really liked Nick. Liked him as a friend, but it went deeper in a way I could not fathom or even understand. The world just seemed a brighter place when he was there.

"We'll be fine," I assured him. "I won't go where it's crowded. I want to take him up the lane past the farm, to see where it ends."

"That old cattle driver's road?" Nick gave a shrug. "I think it goes on forever. Make sure you don't get lost!"

Laughing, I went to the field for Dreamcatcher.

He came trotting up at my call, head high and tail pluming. "Hello boy," I said fondly, slipping on his halter. "Here's your mint. Good?"

He rolled the treat around in his mouth and munched on it, shaking his head at its sharp taste, stretching his neck and hawing lustily to cool down his air passages. Holly whinnied to us from the adjoining paddock, and Dreamcatcher flung up his head and made one of his awful faces at her.

"Stop that! Come on. Let's get you ready."

Soon afterwards we were retracing the steps I'd taken

on Bassy, this time at a hard canter, with the air brushing my face and Dreamcatcher putting in an occasional buck for fun. We went whizzing through Black Woods, jumping streams as I bent over in the saddle to avoid the low overhanging branches. Out again in the brightness, Dreamcatcher put his head down and took the hill at a gallop. We reached the farm in a rush, scattering hens in every direction. There was no sign of Connor, but Polly was there, huge and black, delivering a breathy nicker as we shot by. I remembered that Connor had taken Gyp up into the hills to check the flock, as dipping time was imminent and he needed to be sure they had not strayed.

Once past the farm I sat down in the saddle and eased up on Dreamcatcher's mouth, feeling him come back to me as his gallop slowed to a canter, became a trot and then a springy, snorting walk.

Now on unknown territory, I continued at the slower pace, enjoying the cooling breeze that ruffled Dreamcatcher's mane and fanned my hot cheeks. We followed the trail that today was all too clear of prints, up and up, the way becoming starker and more rugged as we traveled deeper into the hills. Gorse shrubs splashed the slopes with gold, and high above a buzzard circled idly in the blue. We passed one derelict farmstead and then another, both little more than ruins, no longer anybody's home.

At last we came to a small cottage. By the door, a woman in jeans and a baggy paint-smeared smock sat at an artist's easel, daubing away in watercolors at a stunning landscape. Thinking she could be a likely candidate for Lucy's shop, I made a mental note to mention it when I got back and reined in to ask some questions.

"Annie Shone?" the artist repeated, and then shook her head. "No, sorry."

At the next dwelling, a low-roofed, weather-battered farmhouse, an elderly man was tinkering with a tractor in the yard. Here I had a more positive response, and more thought provoking, too.

"Wheel prints?" The farmer denied all knowledge, but I hadn't missed the wariness that had leaped to his faded old eyes as I asked my question. He asked where I was from and what I was doing so far from home. "Go home, girl. Forget it," was his parting shot as I rode away.

We were very high up now. Far below, the village was no more than a smudge beside the sparkling ribbon of the river. I could see all the twinkling little streams, the silver glint of a lake, and the white dots of sheep on the green flanks of the hillsides. I could even see Connor, a minute figure, sending Gyp to circle the flock. I could see everything except what I had come to find.

At last I drew my reins. Ahead, the stony and pitted road wound on its lonely way. There was no sign of Annie's house, and no hint of a horse and buggy. Nothing.

Deflated, I turned Dreamcatcher toward home.

It seemed further going back. A wind blew up, chasing the clouds across the sky and obliterating the sun. The landscape was flung into shadow and looked bleak and inhospitable. I was glad to see the huddle of buildings that was Cross Hill in the dip ahead, and gladder still when we reached Black Woods, and then – oh joy! – the welcome normality of the solid road and reassuring trickle of traffic.

"Hi," said Nick as we clopped into the yard. "How was he?"

"Fine," I replied, dismounting stiffly and giving Dreamcatcher's shoulder a pat. He'd lathered up during the gallop and my hand came away sticky with half-dried sweat. "You were right about the old lane, Nick. It goes too far to cover in one day."

Lucy, a cat weaving around her legs, emerged from the cottage saying I had been gone for ages, and that while I'd been gone, the person who ran the fashion business for her had emailed some exciting news. "It's a new contract with a big retailer. This is so great! Remember that trip to the accountant I mentioned? When I make it, I need to visit the workshops as well and sign some papers. I was wondering, Tessa. Is Wednesday all right with you?"

"Yes." I was suddenly breathless. Here was my chance. Today had been a complete loss. Maybe the smithy would tell me what I wanted to know. "Wednesday's fine."

"I imagine we'll be gone for quite a while. The accountant was drawing up some figures for me for the craft shop. It's a pity we haven't had more local interest."

I told Lucy about the woman in the hills. She seemed pleased.

"A watercolor artist? That sounds interesting. Thanks, Tessa. It might be worth following up. See you Wednesday, then?"

I nodded. Wednesday could not come quickly enough.

* * * *

Wednesday dawned with thick swirls of mist wreathing up from all the damp little hollows on the hillside. The valley swam in milky vapor. My sneakers were soaked by the time I had let out the hens and gathered the eggs.

Bassy's heavy steps were muted as we headed off, passing through banks of foggy clouds that would thin unexpectedly, revealing snatches of a dripping world and then closing in again, a silver cobweb folding around us.

Black Woods went by, Bassy giving astonished little snorts at the changed and silent place he traveled through.

At the end of the lane, road and cottage were hidden behind a silver-gray shroud. Bassy, having gotten his bearings, swung onto the solid surface of the road with a loud clopping of hooves that echoed eerily all the way there.

"Dratted fog!" moaned Lucy, dressed for town and hovering uncertainly by her SUV. "Just when I wanted an early start, too! Let's hope it clears once we get out of the hills."

She shouted for Nick, who materialized from the direction of the stables. "I was just checking a label on a rug. Hi, Tessa. You okay?"

"I'm fine," I said, dismounting. "What time do you plan to get back?"

"Early evening. Say… around six?" Lucy fumbled in her bag for her car keys. "You know where everything is, don't you? Don't worry about the phone. I'll deal with any calls another time. No Gyp today?"

"No. Connor needed him. They're bringing in the sheep for dipping."

"Better him than me," Nick said. "The fog'll be worse up in the hills. If you're feeling energetic, Tessa, the stalls need to be mucked out. The straw's by the stable wall."

"I can take a hint!" I parried. "I might ride Dreamcatcher later."

"Sure. Don't worry about the other two. They can have a day off."

"Your lunch is in the fridge. There's salad and cold cuts. Help yourself to whatever else is in there." Lucy checked her briefcase for the papers for the accountant. "That's everything, I think. Okay, Nick, let's go. 'Bye, Tessa."

I watched them leave the yard, to be immediately swallowed up by the fog. Standing there with Bassy's reins looped over my arm, listening to the car accelerating cautiously away down the road, I shot a speculative glance at the shuttered, mist-shrouded smithy.

Later, I thought. The whole day lay ahead of me. There was plenty of time to carry out my plan. And clicking my tongue at Bassy, I led him into his stall.

I diligently set to work, mucking out, laying fresh straw, replenishing hayracks and water buckets. All done, I collected the tack and went for Dreamcatcher. Answering my hail with a friendly squeal, he came pounding up out of the blanketing cloud, his splotchy coat pearled with moisture. After saddling him, I swung up and sat there a moment, unsure of where to go.

The mist still clung, still hid the sun, so instead of chancing the roads I opted for the fields of the cross-country course. Tweed's and Holly's whinnies floated desolately through the woolly whiteness as I pushed open the field gate and rode through, Dreamcatcher dancing a little at the prospect of something different.

Visibility here seemed better. Instead of the cold impenetrable barrier there was movement, the shapes of trees and hedges growing ever clearer as a spear of gold broke through, the radiance growing in response to the challenging power of the sun.

"Come on, Dreamcatcher," I whispered, and sitting tight I steered him toward the low brush that was fence number one. He flew over it without his hooves seeming to leave the ground. Galloping on, fighting for his head, he took the next jump, a narrow ditch, and then a low stone wall. The jumps were not difficult but this was a young untrained horse and his judgment could not have been better.

Pulling up at the boundary hedge, I glanced back… only to find the cottage and paddocks still oddly curtained off by mist. I stared at it, frowning, uneasy with what I saw. Impatient, Dreamcatcher began to fidget so we took the course a second time, jumping the ditch in both directions because he liked it.

After a while I turned him toward home, walking to cool him down, Tweed and Holly whinnying a shrill welcome out of the woolly grayness.

Indoors at last, having checked on Bassy – who was sleeping, head down, and bottom lip slack – and fed the cat, I thought about grabbing something to eat. The food Lucy had prepared looked delicious, but suddenly I couldn't manage to eat a morsel. At the other end of the building, the smithy waited. It was now or never.

After drinking some juice, I left the half-empty carton on the table and went out to the shed where Nick kept his tools. Tishy followed me, mewing plaintively as I selected a crowbar and sturdy hammer.

Standing in front of the smithy, I threw a glance around. If anything, the mist had intensified. Dense, all-enveloping vapor now covered the road. The fields and distant village were completely lost to sight. A farm truck cruised by, fog lamps blazing, and disappeared again into the murk, leaving a silence so profound that I could hear the nervous beating of my own heart. Somehow, the boarded-up entrance had taken on sinister proportions and I hesitated, of two minds whether to proceed. Curiosity won.

Starting at the top, wincing at every splintering noise, I removed the planks one by one, taking care to stack them in the correct order for replacing. No one must know what I had been doing. No one.

I realized my hands were sweating on the crowbar. About halfway down the entrance, struggling with a particularly thick section of timber, I caught sight of something that sent the tool crashing from my grip. Nailed to the battered wooden door of the smithy was a circlet of tiny images – mummified snouts and paws complete with sharp little claws of woodland creatures that had lived long ago. Peering closer, I identified a mouse, a squirrel, a rat, and maybe a fox. My heart thumped crazily. My mouth was dry.

Who had put them here? And why?

Tempted to board the door up again and forget about the whole thing, I thought again. I was almost finished. I just had to take a peek inside. So keeping my distance from those freaky little body parts, I removed the rest of the planks. There was a moment of panic that the doors might be locked, but when I lifted the rusted latch, the two big doors yielded and swung open with a loud creak of protest.

With my breath held, I stepped inside to dank dimness, taking in the scamper of rodent feet and the stale smell of a place long closed up. It was like stepping back in time, for once my eyes had adapted to the gloom it was apparent that the smithy was exactly as it had been left all those years ago when it been closed down. Dried manure lay in dusty crumbling heaps on the cobbled floor. Close to the boarded-up window was the anvil, securely mounted on its solid block of wood to absorb shocks. Beside it, the big heavy sledgehammer and the lighter one for nailing shoes lay abandoned, as if the smith had dropped them there and skipped out on an errand.

The area was smaller and more cramped than I expected,

the roof lower and criss-crossed with rafters dressed with ancient cobwebs and thick with decades of dust. Hanging from nails on the beams were sets of shoes for plough horses and ponies, and forging tools of every kind. Identifying three forge tools – a fuller, a flatter and a swage – I moved on. At the back of the room, the long-dead furnace was blackened and cold, the fat chimney no longer carrying off smoke. But standing conveniently was a wooden pail for holding water to cool the white-hot metal, and on a ledge above was a pewter tankard and an ale jug waiting to quench a driving thirst.

Wonderingly I took in the array of fire tongs, each sporting a different shaped jaw designed to hold the metal firmly when working at the anvil. Each was perfect. Useable. An unchanged craft in a drastically changed world.

Directly under the window ran a stout wooden workbench with several vises, the top littered with small tools, files and chisels, all of them coated with dust and vermin droppings. Shelves lined the opposite wall, filled with boxes of rusting nails and screws, and snaking from pegs were lengths of heavy metal chain. In a far corner a harrow stood ready for fettling. Closer, strewn about the floor at my feet, were various odds and ends – a set of new shoes, iron bars and other discarded items that can lie about for ages and suddenly come in handy. There were metal rings in the walls for tying up horses, piles of worn shoes waiting to be melted down for reuse… everything was at hand, ready for the smith to resume work. Only he hadn't, had he?

I stood there, taking it all in, pondering what might have happened here to bring a perfectly working forge to such an unprecedented stop. And as I lingered there, a strange sensation came over me, as if I were not alone. Skin prickling, I swung around, breath catching in my throat.

"Who is it?" I whispered. "Who's there?"

In the shadows a deeper shadow flickered as if in response, and clamoring on the air currents was a terrible yearning that verged on desperation. Noises came and went. The scrape of an iron-shod hoof on stone, a swift impatient blowing through wide nostrils… voices. The sounds came from a long way off… were there and yet not there… and I strained my ears, trying to make sense of what I heard.

And then a very real shape scampered alongside the wall and vanished down a hole with a flick of a ratty tail, bringing me starkly back to reality. The sour stink of the place was suddenly overpowering. Whatever was going on here, whatever it was trying to tell me, I didn't want to know, and I turned and stumbled out into the damp of the sunless summer day.

"Phew!" Passing a rubbery hand across my face, I gulped in quantities of soggy air and waited for the trembling to subside. It was more normal out here. The smithy looked like what it was – a run-down old workplace badly in need of care and attention, and I was able to scold myself for my overreaction. My fear was irrational. A building shut up for so long was bound to be freaky, wasn't it?

Almost convinced, my eyes darted again to the opening of the abandoned blacksmith's shop. It looked darker now. There was a waiting silence.

In that moment the quiet was split by a ragged whinny that I recognized as Dreamcatcher's. Bassy, abruptly awakened in his stall, answered him. Dreamcatcher shrieked again and the other two horses joined in. All three began galloping around and around their paddocks with a pounding that hammered menacingly through the fog.

"Hey, you guys! Stop that!" I yelled, and shooting the smithy one more confused glance I ran to see what was the matter. The horses were still charging wildly around and, grabbing some feed from the store, I stood at the gate, rattling the bucket enticingly and clicking my tongue to them, hoping to ease their distress.

"Holly, Tweed, whoa there. Come on, Dreamcatcher. Good boy."

Dreamcatcher came racing up and skidded to a halt in front of me, his eyes wild, nostrils flaring, and flesh still quivering in alarm. He dipped his nose in the feed but threw up his head again, listening, grains of oats and barley clinging to his whiskers. Sea Holly and Rough Tweed had gone to the farthest corner of the paddock and stood like wraiths in the shifting veils of fog, very close together, their gaze riveted on the gaping mouth of the smithy. Neither was interested in the untimely treat. Dreamcatcher, wrenching his gaze away, peered at me through stormy, uncomprehending eyes. In the stable yard Bassy had his head over the door of his stall, but he too refused the food and looked mildly troubled, his flanks heaving as if he had been pushed too hard between the shafts.

"There now. Come on. What a fuss you're all making over nothing."

The scared wobble in my voice did nothing to calm the horses' nerves and set my own jangling. Soberly I returned to the smithy and began the process of re-boarding the entrance. A breeze blew in as I worked, driving away the fog. The village on the lower road reappeared magically, hedges and rooftops glistening in the breaking sunlight.

Job done, I returned the tools to the shed. The horses had now recovered their calm and were grazing quietly. Bassy still stood at the door of the stall but was idly watching the swallows as they swooped for flies around the eaves of the cottage, his old placid self once more.

Everything seemed as it should be and my stomach responded to the release from tension with a healthy growl of hunger. But my problems were not quite over. In the kitchen I noticed that Tishy was not in her usual spot by the stove. A search of the cottage revealed her at last, curled up under Lucy's bed, rigid with fright, tail wrapped around her body as if to protect her. Unlike the horses, Tishy allowed herself to be wooed by the offer of food. She ate delicately, gave herself a top-to-tail grooming and left by the cat-flap in the door. It was the last I saw of her that day.

I was washing the lunch dishes when Nick called to say they expected to be back by five at the latest.

"How was the trip?" I asked him.

"Great. There was no fog after we left Rydale. Is everything okay with you?"

"Great," I fibbed. "The time's flown."

"That's a surprise." Nick's trusting laugh burned on my ears. "I bet you've been wearing out Dreamcatcher's shoes on the road. So who's paying for his next set?"

The jest was too close to home for comfort, and when he hung up I set about tidying up the kitchen, mopping the floor, and whatever else it took to ease my guilty conscience. Regret at having tampered with something I shouldn't have was starting to gnaw at me.

The rest of the day passed uneventfully. Lucy and Nick returned and I went to tack up Bassy for home. A dried white crusting of sweat remained on Bassy's russet-brown flanks and quarters, which I removed hastily with a stable rubber. I wanted to get away from the creepy forge with its baffling secret and horrid little effigies on the door. I wanted the reassuring solidness of Cross Hill, and Connor whistling to himself as he made the rounds of the farm. But once on the old lane, I was in for yet another shock. The tracks were here again! There were no wheel marks this time; simply the churned, unmistakable indentations of galloping hooves, and leading not toward the smithy but away from it, as if whatever had been confined there was now running free.

And when I reached Black Woods, a figure stood waiting for me in the rustling shadows of the trees.

CHAPTER SIX

"Have you seen the horse?" Annie asked sharply.

She looked agitated and I was instantly on my guard. Before, when I had mentioned the ubiquitous tracks, she had gone scarily inward-looking and strange… and I had had enough for one day. So I feigned indifference and shook my head. "I don't think so, Annie. The only horse here is Bassy."

For a moment I thought my ruse had failed. Annie kept on peering up and down the path, as if she expected what she was seeking to come leaping out of the bushes at any moment. When it didn't she seemed reassured, fixing me with a more rational gaze.

"I'm glad you've turned up, Tessa. You know these treatments and remedies of mine you're so taken with? I've had an idea. What if I tell you all I know and you write it down in a book? You'll have a record, then."

Normally I would have jumped at her offer. As it was… "Well, that sounds great, but –"

"There's no time like the present." Annie was not about to be brushed off. "Let's start with the eye problem."

Resigned, I dismounted and tethered Bassy to a tree. Annie began rummaging around in the undergrowth at the side of the path, looking for chickweed. Pouncing on a clump, she yanked it up jubilantly.

"This is the stuff. You add about this much to a jug of hot water and leave it to distil until it's cold. Strain it off, and that's your treatment. Easy."

"I see."

As she had suspected, my interest was fired. Her eyes sharpened cunningly. "You need to dry what you can't use," she said, transferring the chickweed to her basket. "Never let anything go to waste. Dried leaves and roots are twice as strong as fresh, remember. You must use only half the quantities or you could be in for trouble."

"Some plants are poisonous when they're dried. Like ragwort," I conceded.

"That's right. Never overdo it is a good rule of thumb. You're a quick learner, Tessa. Help me pick some more. Two pairs of hands are better than one."

I did as she asked. There was no point arguing with Annie.

We worked companionably at filling the basket with what I called herbs but she referred to as weeds. Sometimes she required the flower heads only. Other times it was just the sappy leaves or the root. As we picked she gave a rapid commentary on what this was for and how that worked, and before long my head started to swim.

"Stop!" I cried. "I'll never be able to remember it all!"

Annie chuckled affably and said I would, given time. We were getting along so well that I almost dismissed my earlier caution and confided what had happened at the smithy. But didn't it make a thing more real, more threatening, when you put it into words? So I held back. I didn't even mention going in search of where she lived, but instead gave myself up to the soothing task of gathering herbs in the mossy reaches of the woods.

When at last I mounted up for the final leg home, I saw that the hoofprints had begun to fade, and by the time I reached Cross Hill they were gone.

"Did you have a good day?" asked Connor as I untacked in the yard.

"Yes, thanks," I replied, noncommittal.

When I removed the bridle, all too evident were the whitish sweat marks that I in my haste had failed to remove from Bassy's head. And Connor frowned.

"He's been in a lather. What happened?"

"Nothing much. He got a little wound up in the stall."

"Bassy did?" Connor snorted. "Come on! He doesn't know how!"

"The other horses were tearing around. He probably wanted to join them," I said as nonchalantly as I could. "You're back early. Did you bring the sheep down?"

"Yes, that's all done. They're in the barn ready for the men tomorrow, aren't they, Gyp?" Connor bent to fuss over the dog and commented that he was the best sheep dog he'd ever trained, and the nicest. "I was about to go out to the supermarket and stock up on supplies. Want to come?"

Normally I would have refused, but a mundane jaunt to the shopping center seemed like a perfect antidote to the nerve-jangling events of the day – and I needed a notebook for Annie's remedies. So I ran to grab my purse.

On the way there in the farm truck, Connor asked how Dreamcatcher was coming along and if I thought he'd make the eventing scene.

"He's sure to," I said. "All Dreamcatcher lacks is size, and Nick's tall. There's a chance he may feel under-horsed after Sea Holly and Rough Tweed."

"Couldn't you ride for him?" Connor suggested, his eyes on the road ahead.

"No. I'm not into competition riding."

"I can't say I blame you. I enjoy a day out at a show, but apart from that I'm happy for the horses to be working guys. I imagine you're the same with their schooling. I must say

I'm glad that you've found something to occupy your time. I was afraid you'd be bored stuck here all summer. Nothing much goes on in Rydale."

That was the understatement of the day!

We turned into the shopping complex where most of Cross Hill's household requirements were met and Connor parked the truck, complaining because there was no spot close to the entrance. The supermarket was one of those super stores that stocks everything from television sets to garden accessories and clothing. From the stationery section I chose an attractive hard-backed notebook with a pattern of leaves and flowers on the cover, and some colored pens.

There was an interesting book and audio-visual display, so while Connor toured the aisles with shopping list and cart, I scanned the shelves for something on local history and the Old Forge. Nothing turned up so, leaving my purchases with Connor, I went out into the shopping mall, located a second-hand bookshop and had more luck. There was a slim volume entitled *Curiosities of Rydale – Fact or Fiction*, which I bought.

Back in the supermarket, I found Connor at the register behind a full cart, dolefully unloading packs of breakfast cereals and items for the freezer.

"Who'd have thought two people could go through so much food?" he moaned, mocking an air of abject grieving. "I don't buy stuff like this when it's just me."

"That's just because you don't eat properly," I returned. "I bet you live on junk food and fried stuff."

"You're right about that, Tessa. It's a good thing you came along to put me on the right track!"

The new camaraderie stirred a pleasant warmth inside me and banished the last traces of unquiet from the day. The nice feeling was still there later as I went yawning to bed.

Then it vanished totally.

Settling down against the pillows, I reached for the book. It fell open at a page of early photographs, the sepia-colored kind where the long, long exposure makes the expressions of the subjects look fixed and staring. Glancing at them, I let out a gasp. For here was a shot of the Old Forge, the smithy newly boarded up, by the look of it. Underneath was the caption: Local Tradesman Pays The Price For Devil Horse!

Feverishly I searched the printed page for more. There wasn't much. A horse was said to have killed a blacksmith while being shod and his wife, in an attempt to restrain the animal, had struck her head against the wall and perished also. The horse had galloped off in fright and was never seen again, and this despite rigorous attempts to find it. With two people dead, the Old Forge now had bad associations and no one was willing to take over the business. Sightings of ghostly horse tracks and a carriage were reported, putting yet another cloud over a village that had been thriving and happy. The people of Rydale, fearing a loss of revenue, made the decision to board up the smithy and never to speak again of what had happened.

The article ended with the question as to whether the story was true or false. And of course the conclusion veered to the latter. The author commented on the remarkable power that superstition and irrational fear held over mankind and how the imagination can play tricks on even the most pragmatic.

The book shook slightly in my hand. I thought of the opened smithy that had been shut away for a specific purpose. The shadowy shapes, the cold – now understandable – sense of horror and the puzzling desperation that had cried out to be noticed. The way Dreamcatcher and the other horses had reacted… the little tortoiseshell cat cowering under the bed. Even the fog, cloying and sinister.

Everyone at Rydale, from the long established to the newly arrived, had respected the decision of that earlier community and left the smithy alone, so that it had become a tradition to be honored and upheld. Until I had come along.

Why oh why had I taken things so rashly into my own hands?

There was no answer, no solace. Putting the book aside, I turned off the light and eventually slept, only to dream of a sinister whispering – *devil horse, devil horse* – and a road along which a spirited horse galloped between the shafts of a high-wheeled carriage, on and on, never to reach its journey's end.

CHAPTER SEVEN

Heavy-eyed and yawning after a night of broken sleep,
I rode along with Gyp bounding in front, the white tip of
his tail bobbing. This morning the sun was shining and
the ground showed only the deep dinner-plate imprints
of Bassy's passage the previous day. We thudded through
Black Woods at a sedate plod and continued between the
high banks of the sunken byway to the road.

Upon reaching our destination, Gyp dropped to the
ground with a puzzled whine, his gaze fixed on the
shuttered entrance to the smithy. At the same time Bassy
jibbed, eyes rolling in alarm.

"Get on," I said, nudging.

Bassy responded with a stubborn flick of the tail and dug
in his heels. I used my legs, shook the reins, and shouted,
but nothing would make the big horse move forward.
Touched by a disturbing image of a hidden circlet of freaky
remains on the battered old door only inches from where we
stood, I dismounted, dug in my pocket for the Polo mints
and shoved the entire pack under Bassy's nose to tempt
him. Surrendering, he came at a reluctant stamping walk,
flesh twitching and tail thrashing uneasily. Once clear of
the entrance he reverted to his usual affable self and stood
repentant, peering at me bemusedly through a straggling
forelock. A small, embarrassed snort escaped his nostrils.

"I should think so!" I admonished him, turning to Gyp
who still lay flattened to the pavement. "Gyp – come!"

At the command the collie sprang obediently to his feet, but instead of chancing the smithy and whatever horrors it held for him, he whipped around and went streaking off the way we had come, his tail rammed between his legs.

"Gyp! Come back!" I hollered, and putting my fingers to my lips I attempted one of Connor's piercing whistles that normally brought the dog to heel but this time had no effect. The shouting and commotion brought Lucy and Nick running from the cottage demanding to know what was wrong.

"Gyp's run off," I gasped, thrusting Bassy's reins at Nick. "I'm going after him."

"I'll come too," Lucy offered.

Together we pounded along the road, pulling to a stop at the entrance to the old lane to peer hopefully up it. There was no sign of the dog.

"He's probably run home," Lucy said. She shook her head wordlessly and looked annoyed. "These animals! I don't know what's gotten into them all of a sudden. That goes for Tishy as well, and she's usually no trouble at all."

"Why?" Unease frisked through me. "What do you mean?"

"She seems to be missing. I've called and called but she hasn't come. The others are just being stupid and acting up. Tweed almost threw Nick off when he rode him bareback in the field as he always does. And Holly's apparently in a state over nothing. It's crazy!"

Yesterday's wild galloping and gentle Bassy, coated in sweat, sprang to mind. I thought of the message between the pages of the book and felt that cold ache of misgiving. Biting my lip, I recalled the dream that had prowled in my sleep and wakened me in heart-thumping panic.

Devil horse! Devil horse!

What had I done?

"I've got to find Gyp. Connor will never forgive me if anything happens to him."

"I wouldn't worry too much," Lucy said consolingly. "Gyp's probably home by now. Come and have a snack. Maybe Tishy will have turned up."

The cat had not, and when Nick came in from the yard he was not in the best mood.

"Your Dreamcatcher's just tried to take a bite out of me. He missed, luckily."

"Bad horse!" Lucy muttered.

"Dreamcatcher isn't. He wouldn't do it deliberately," I said in swift defense.

"Well, he just did." Nick's mouth made a rueful downward quirk. "They're all in bad moods today. Maybe some road work would help."

"That's a good idea. We could go and look for Gyp."

"Have you called the farm?" Nick asked.

"There's no point. They're dipping today. Connor will be with them. It's useless trying his cell phone. The signal's iffy at Cross Hill."

"In that case we'll ride that way."

Nick downed a cup of tea in a few scalding gulps and went out to saddle his horse. Leaving my drink unfinished, I followed to do the same. Dreamcatcher was not himself at all, refusing to keep still, flattening his ears evilly when I latched up the girth, and lifting a threatening hoof.

"Don't you even think about it!" I scolded. "Stand. Be good."

Mounted at last, we left Lucy searching the paddocks for her little cat and rode off, Tweed sulking and unresponsive,

86

and Dreamcatcher skittering irritatingly. The river charged downward today belligerently. Even the streams that trickled across the path seemed less harmless than usual. Hostile, somehow.

"It must have been raining up in the hills last night," Nick remarked, urging Tweed up to his bit. "The river rises there. It's always high if the rainfall's heavy. Oh, stop lagging, Tweed! What's wrong with you today? Let's gallop, Tessa, and open them up a bit."

We gave the horses their heads and went thundering uphill toward the farm. At Cross Hill the air reeked of a chemical smell and rang with the indignant bleating of sheep and the shouts of the men. Connor, breaking off to see what we wanted, listened gravely to my explanation.

"Gyp's not here," he said, frowning. "I wonder what made him run? It's not like him."

"I know. We'll try the pasture. He could be there."

"Don't worry," Nick added. "We'll find him."

"I hope so." Connor's frown deepened. "It's typical, me being tied up here when I want to come with you."

We pressed on up into the hills, whistling for the dog, calling, calling, until our voices croaked and we could call no more. I kept hoping to see Gyp's lithe black and white form come bounding toward us, with his tongue lolling and tail quivering repentantly. It did not happen.

"This is useless." Nick pulled up and sat gazing around at the expanse of open land. "Gyp could be anywhere. He goes with Connor to the forest, doesn't he? He could have bolted in there. Do you want to look?"

"We could," I conceded woodenly.

We were quiet as we rode back, the horses' hooves slithering on the rough trail, dislodging sand and tiny stones and sending them showering downhill. At the farm, Connor stopped working the dipping gate to cup his hands to his mouth and holler out, asking if had we had any success. Nick shook his head emphatically, and Connor shrugged and turned back to the sheep.

A search along the forest edge proved equally fruitless. The same harrowing thought must have been in both our minds – and Connor's too. A stray dog in sheep country was at the mercy of any farmer's gun. It was the unwritten code of the countryside. The flocks had to be protected no matter what. The notion of that bright life being snuffed out brought an ache of unshed tears to my throat.

Nick nudged Tweed alongside Dreamcatcher and took my hand in his. "Try not to worry. It wasn't your fault. All the animals are acting weird today. Maybe it's something elemental, like a full moon. It can have an affect."

"I know. Our neighbor back home has a cat that yowls terribly whenever there's a full moon," I said in a small voice. His hand tightened on mine and something caught at me, poignant and unexpected. It was as if the dark and gloomy forest had become sprinkled with a golden magic of happiness.

Nick sent me a lopsided grin. "I suggest we go home and grab something to eat. And just hope the cat's turned up."

Lucy's woebegone face as we clopped into the yard told its own story. Giving me a wink of encouragement, Nick silently took Dreamcatcher's reins and saw to both horses, while I went inside to help prepare a belated lunch.

"Tishy's never stayed away this long before," Lucy sighed, grating cheese for sandwiches. "She wasn't here yesterday when we came in, but she often goes on long treks and I thought nothing of it. Can you remember when you last saw her?"

"Late afternoon when I fed her. She went out soon afterwards."

"That's what she usually does. Oh well, I guess she'll come back when she's ready. It's odd about Gyp, though. Dogs run home as a rule."

"Yes." I swallowed hard. "Do you think the authorities should be notified?"

"Possibly. I would leave that to Connor." Lucy transferred the sandwiches onto a plate. "There, that's done. Would you give Nick a call, Tessa."

None of us were very talkative during the meal. My guilt was growing. Things had gone desperately wrong here and I could be the cause. Even as I thought it, common sense intervened. What I had done could not possibly be connected with today's scenario. Could it?

It was that tiny seed of doubt that dug into my thoughts. Something bad had happened here at the Old Forge. People had reacted by closing it down. And I had flown in the face of fate and opened it up again. Would I have done it had I known the history behind the boarded-up blacksmith's shop? I didn't think so!

After the usual stable chores I took off, back to a very troubled Connor who starkly rejected the idea of supper and left to look for his dog.

The tears that had threatened now welled and spilled over helplessly. I sat at the scrubbed kitchen table, cradled my head in my arms and gave way to a bout of sobbing that left me physically drained and more miserable than ever.

Perhaps, I thought, I should have come clean about what I had done and risked the consequences. It could cause a broken trust and the shattering of friendships. The magical bond with Nick would be gone, Lucy would think less of me, and as for Connor… he'd blame me for losing his dog. Worse still was the prospect that I might never ride Dreamcatcher again.

I was reaching for a fresh tissue when the phone rang. At first I left it. The caller could be my mother. I'd never trick Mom into thinking that all was well. Then again, if I didn't respond she'd only worry. At the tenth ring I snatched it up.

"Yes?"

"Hello, Tessa," said a very familiar voice.

For several moments everything stopped; the ticking of the long-cased clock on the wall, the soft sifting of coals in the range, even the ragged breath in my body. Then, "Dad!" I gasped. "Dad, it's you! Oh, wow!"

"Surprised?"

"Of course I am. It's been such a long time." Anger spurted, sharp, abrasive. "Dad, I've been so worried. Why haven't you been in touch? I've missed you. I thought… I thought you didn't care any more."

"Oh, Tessa. You know better than that," Dad said reproachfully. "Remember that little problem I had with my eyes? I've had it fixed."

"You've had surgery?" All my anger dispersed. "Dad, I'm sorry. I should have come and visited."

"It would have been a long trip, Tessa. I had to come north to have it done. I was warned about how long the healing would take, which is partly why I hadn't bothered before."

"Are you recovered? Was it a success?"

"Very much so and I'm feeling great. Never better. I hope to be back home soon and then we can arrange a visit. Now, that's enough about me. What's your news? How are you really, Tessa?"

"I'm fine Dad," I said quickly. Too quickly, and Dad wasn't fooled.

"Tessa, don't play games with me. What's wrong?"

"It's complicated."

"Problems often are. I'm all ears, if you want to tell me."

"Well… Dad, do you believe in the supernatural?" I blurted.

"Ah." There was a pause. "Now that depends. Maybe you should start at the beginning."

So I told him. I told him everything. About meeting Nick and Lucy and riding Dreamcatcher, and the tracks and the events surrounding the Old Forge. I told him, shamefully, about my part in the whole sorry muddle and how I had kept it from the Merediths. Dad listened, not interrupting, letting me take my time. I could picture his thin, clever face intent behind the phone, the hand that held it steady and reassuring.

At last I came to a faltering stop. "That's about it, Dad. I wish I'd come clean with Lucy and Nick. Not telling them has made things worse and I don't know what to do."

"Oh, I think you'll do the right thing, Tessa," Dad said with gentle confidence. There was another pause, and then he went on, "It's a curious business."

"About the smithy? It certainly is! It was so freaky in there. I had this weird feeling of being watched. And then the scene seemed to change. It did, Dad. I swear it. Do you think it's possible to get snatches of the past?"

"Who can say? I suppose it depends on whether you've crossed the stream."

Dad's words tweaked a memory. Annie. Annie Shone had said something similar. She talked in riddles too. "What's that supposed to mean?" I said despondently.

"It's largely a term used by people who claim they can see into the past, but it has other meanings too. I'm not saying they can't. It's good to keep an open mind about these things. What you have to remember is that decades ago, when that place was closed up, people were more swayed by superstitious belief than they are today. It wouldn't have taken much to set them off; just, say… a runaway horse and buggy on the lane, coupled with what happened to the unfortunate smith and his wife. Then someone puts two and two together and makes five, everyone gets fired up, and there you have it. They decide the Old Forge is bad news, and say, 'Let's shut it down.'"

"You mean there could be nothing to it?"

"It's a consideration. I bet many a so-called haunting can be explained away with a little hindsight." I heard Dad's doorbell ring. He said, "I have to go, Tessa. We'll talk again. If you need me I can be reached at this number."

Gratefully, I scribbled it down. Dad sent his best wishes to Mom and we said goodbye.

I felt cheered as I set the phone back in its cradle. Knowing that Dad was there for me again, sharing my problems with him, made things seem a whole lot better. My troubles were starting to recede.

Having just about convinced myself that the mystery of the smithy was nothing more than a load of gloomy drama cooked up by people from a less well-informed age, I went outside and fed the horses and saw to the other tasks usually undertaken by Connor. From the barn came the forlorn bleating of sheep fretting for the freedom of the hills.

"Cheer up! You'll be back there soon enough," I called out to them.

Indoors once more, still optimistic, I started preparing

92

dinner. My new-found optimism crashed dramatically when Connor returned without Gyp.

"There's no trace, and I have no clue where he can be." Connor dropped himself wearily into a chair. His clothes were stained and rumpled from the day's work and he stank of sheep and chemicals. Running a grimy fist across his forehead, leaving a smudge, he fixed me with a troubled gaze. "Tell me exactly what happened."

I did more than that. Sliding the dinner pans off the burners, I sat down opposite him and repeated everything I had told Dad. Connor listened as Dad had done, saying little, hearing me out to the very end.

"Huh," he exclaimed then. "You sure have stirred things up!"

"What do you mean?" I stared at him, incredulous. "You don't actually believe this crazy myth? A killer horse, the forge being bad news? You do, don't you? That's why you got so mad at me for switching the brass pieces on the bridles. You really think those flashes can protect against evil forces."

Connor looked faintly abashed. "Let's say I'm not one to tempt fate. There're many things that can't be rationalized."

"That's not what Dad said."

"No. Well, I wouldn't begin to argue with someone as knowledgeable as your father. Is psychic phenomena his area?"

"Not exactly. Dad's a geologist."

"I see. There's a little difference. Why don't you just keep away from the Meredith place?"

"I can't. There's Dreamcatcher. I'm schooling him."

"There are other horses, Tessa. I'll see if there's one we can lease for you."

I shook my head. "It wouldn't be the same. Besides, Nick and Lucy are my friends."

"They might not be so chummy once they know what you've been up to," Connor said darkly. He sighed. "This isn't getting us anywhere. Is that supper I smell? Let's eat, and then I need to get the flock back to the hills. Since I don't have a sheepdog to help, you might as well lend a hand."

Chastened, I went to serve the meal. I had been responsible for Gyp and it was my fault that he was missing. *My fault*. Was I to blame for those other things, too? I wondered if the horses had settled down and if Lucy had been reunited with her cat. Lucy adored Tishy. She'd be devastated if anything had happened to her pet.

Was it really fright that had made them run? It seemed that way to me.

****

Devil horse! Devil horse!

I woke with a yelp of terror to the clamor of galloping hooves and the unmistakable rattle of carriage wheels on the hillside beyond. For a moment I lay still, my heart racing and ears straining. Was what I heard a residue of a nightmare? I could still hear the hoofbeats, or maybe it was the frightened pounding of my own heart.

Mustering courage, I left the bed and went to the window. Moonlight washed the farmyard and landscape with silver. In the field, Bassy and Polly were thundering around and around, the drumbeat of hooves slicing the midnight silence. Gripping the window sill till my knuckles whitened, I scanned the hillside for the horse and carriage. There was nothing, but horrifyingly distinct under the cold light of the full moon were the black lines of carriage wheels on the old lane, and the deep indentations left by

a horse traveling at full pace. My heart jerked in a painful spasm of fear.

Had I really heard those voices? *Devil horse*. It had sounded real, as real as the carriage wheels and galloping horse.

Bassy and Polly stopped charging around and went to roll in the long damp grass by the hedge. The double row of tracks was already fading. It had become very quiet. Around me, the farmhouse slumbered. There was no sound from Connor in his bedroom on the other side of the house, no click-click of claws on the kitchen flagstones below where Gyp would normally be.

Pushing open the window, I leaned out to see if the collie might have turned up and was below waiting to be let in, but the only flicker of life was one of the barn cats, slinking along the fence on a ratting spree.

Going back to bed, I pulled the comforter over my head and went back to sleep, to be wakened it seemed only minutes later by Connor yelling up the back stairs that it was late, the hens were clucking to be let out, and Polly was lame.

CHAPTER EIGHT

Nothing was quite the same after that. Connor was morose and uncommunicative and spent every spare moment combing the countryside for Gyp. On the brighter side, Polly's injury turned out to be nothing more serious than a bruised hoof. Now short a horse as well as a dog, Connor took the usual course of action and rested the mare. But then another chance encounter with Annie put me in touch with arnica to cure the bruise. Unbeknownst to Connor, I went ahead with the treatment. To my delight it appeared to be working.

At the Old Forge, things were not good. Rough Tweed and Sea Holly continued to give Nick trouble – freaking out in the ring, making a shambles of the show jumps, unsettled on the cross-country course. Dreamcatcher wasn't much better. I had to work hard to hold his attention. On one occasion he spooked badly on the lane and took off with me. With muscles stretched to their limit I fought to rein him in, trees and banks whizzing by. We were well past Black Woods before I regained control.

The incident did nothing for my confidence. Was I losing my talent for riding? The question nagged, as did an increasing guilt over what had become my dark secret. If only I had left the smithy alone.

I was often on the verge of confessing my deed to Nick and Lucy, but did not. What would it accomplish? It was done now, the vibes – or whatever was in there – released into the air. Nothing could reverse it. I was better holding on and seeing what each day brought.

Nothing, however, prepared me for what happened when I arrived at the Merediths' place three or four days after Dreamcatcher had bolted with me. Nick was putting Tweed over the show jumps. Most lay on the ground. One of the poles was smashed to matchsticks.

"This is hopeless," Nick said, riding up. Tweed shook his head irritably, resisting the bit. His ears were flattened, his neck and flanks lathered and steaming. "I don't know what's happened here. Holly's the same. Maybe I've pushed them too hard."

Aware of a fresh gnawing of guilt, I tried to be constructive. "Let's put up the jumps and have another try. Tweed could be having an off day."

"It seems to me that every day's an off day lately, but okay," Nick said glumly.

We persevered and managed to get the horse jumping with something close to his old form. We were both relieved when Lucy called us for a morning break. It was a hot day and she brought a tray of cold drinks and the cookie jar out to the courtyard behind the cottage. We were sitting there, taking a break in the bright sunshine, when Nick dropped his bombshell.

"There are only a couple of weeks till the event. I'm seriously thinking of scratching."

We stared at him in shock. I put my glass down with a jerk, spilling some of its contents onto the flagstones. "You can't mean it."

"I just said so, didn't I?"

He spoke with a stark helplessness. The coming event had meant everything to Nick. It was unbelievable that he could give up.

"Nick, you can't." I paused, then went on carefully. "Maybe you were right about the horses being stale. Why not give them a couple of days off and see if it helps?"

"Because they can't afford time off. They need to be kept in form. You know that as well as I do."

Lucy said in a low voice, "Something has happened here to make things go wrong. It's got to have something to do with that." She directed a nod at the smithy end of the cottage.

"That's ridiculous!" said Nick into the silence that followed. He turned to me. "I guess by now you've heard the story behind this place, Tessa?"

"Well… yes." I gave a little shrug. "I read about it in a book."

"Did you?" Nick snorted disparagingly. "It's a lot of nonsense. A tall tale cooked up by some rubes and embellished over the years. We should have done what I suggested and gutted the smithy along with the rest when we were renovating."

"It was my idea not to," Lucy put in. "I wanted us to be accepted here before doing anything… drastic."

"Like opening the smithy up?" I said.

"That's right!" Lucy conceded with a touch of snappishness. "What would you have done?"

"I'm not sure." I chewed on my lip. "I wouldn't give up on the horses."

"Wouldn't you?" Nick gazed at me, cold and distant, his eyes like blue ice. "Okay. Then why not do the event yourself? Dreamcatcher's up to it."

"He might be, but I'm not! I'd fall apart."

"No you wouldn't. Tessa, you're a good rider. You've just got this thing about performing in public. You can overcome it if you try."

99

"I couldn't, I tell you! I'd freeze up and ruin Dreamcatcher's chances for good."

"Stop being so dramatic! You and Dreamcatcher could go right to the top if you'd just snap out of it."

"I couldn't, Nick!"

"Yes you could!"

We wrangled on, the quarrel becoming more ugly and shrill, Nick unusually rude and hurtful, me defensive and embarrassingly close to tears.

"Nick, stop this!" cut in Lucy finally. "If Tessa doesn't feel up for competition riding then that's fair enough. She shouldn't be bullied into it. It's not a priority anyway. What's more important is this property in which we've invested a great deal of time and money. Something's wrong here. I'm concerned about it."

"So what do you suggest?" Nick switched his attack from me to his sister. "We sell it all and move? And that's supposing we can actually get a buyer. They sure saw us coming when we bought the place."

"Nick, we didn't know it had been on the market for so long," Lucy told him, stricken. "It seemed so ideal. We really liked it."

"Of course we did," Nick growled. "We still do. It's got everything we want."

"Plus a history," Lucy reminded him. "If I'd known I might have thought twice about buying. Too bad we weren't informed."

"Too bad you're taking this attitude now. There's nothing wrong with the Old Forge. I don't believe all this talk of bad omens."

"Oh, listen to you!" Lucy shrieked, her control breaking. "You can be so infuriating at times! The evidence is there to see. Those wheel tracks Tessa spoke of. The way the animals are reacting. Tishy hasn't come back and I don't blame her. There's a changed atmosphere here. It's scary. Don't you understand?"

"Lucy, kids on bikes use the lane. The tracks could be made by them. And anything could have freaked the animals into running off, like a car backfiring. Dogs and cats have very acute hearing."

"And the horses? Could they have suddenly become spooked by ordinary everyday noises? Nick, it's not like you to be so blind."

"True," I said before I could stop myself.

Nick rounded on me angrily. "Don't *you* start! We're doing all right here. We've got the goodwill of the man who lets us ride cross-country on his fields. That's fine for starters and it will grow. Now, are we wasting more time talking or do we take the horses out?"

Without another word I finished my drink and stood up. Lucy gathered up the dishes and vanished into the cottage. Nick went to get Sea Holly and I did the same with Dreamcatcher. Once out on our ride we didn't speak much. We had to pass the smithy on our return, and when both horses freaked and almost skittered into a passing car whose driver blasted the horn at us angrily, I was so overcome with remorse that I turned to Nick in desperation.

"Now what?" he snapped, having shot the disappearing vehicle a glower so hot it almost melted the rubber tires.

It had been on the tip of my tongue to confess to my crime but, taken aback by the cold unreasonable anger that haunted Nick's eyes, I was powerless to form the words. "Nothing," I said in a mumble. "Stupid drivers. They should have more sense."

"Oh, well, I guess it's not great having half a ton of horseflesh waving its hooves over your windshield." He paused. "I thought for a moment you were going to take me up on my proposition."

"The one-day event? No way! I still think you should go with Tweed and Holly. It's your last chance this season to qualify for the next stage. You can't turn it down."

"Oh, can't I!" Nick stated bitterly.

For once I was glad to leave the yard and head for home, on foot since Bassy was working on the farm, thanks to Polly still being out of action. I was glad, too, to bump into Annie, gathering watercress on the banks of the stream that flowed through Black Woods. A friendship had sprung up between us. She was teaching me a lot about herbal lore and was a wonderful source of knowledge on natural healing therapy. The more I spoke with her, the more certain I was that this was where my future lay.

"How's the remedy book coming?" Annie wanted to know.

"Fine. I just hope I'm getting it right."

"You will. It's all a matter of understanding, and you don't have a problem there. How's Polly?"

"Much better. She's almost sound again, thanks to you."

"Well, we've got to help each other out, haven't we, Tessa?"

I stared past her at the ancient road that had seen centuries of plodding feet and creaking wheels. The tracks were not there today, but the hateful whispering pounded on in my head.

Devil horse! Devil horse!

"Do you believe that a horse can be born bad?" I asked.

Annie's eyes were on me, bright, inscrutable. She said, "My man used to say there were no bad horses, only bad

102

handlers. He would help anybody out. Especially with horses. He was good with them."

"But what about you? Do you believe that a horse can be born bad?" I persisted.

"Yes, I do," she snapped, making me jump. "I didn't agree with my man. I didn't then and I still don't. He was like that about horses. Wouldn't hear a thing against them – the fool!"

She turned angrily back to the watercress beds and I left her to it. This was the second time Annie had showed a darker side to her nature. I didn't like it and I couldn't get away fast enough.

Nothing was going right, so it was inevitable that my mind turned to Nick and the way he had taunted me. It was unfair of him, I mused as I tramped up the path. Not everyone had Nick's nerveless zest for competition and focus on sporting excellence. Then again, Nick had not been himself today and neither had Lucy. What was happening to us? We had been a happy bunch. How could it all have gone so wrong? And why, added a small voice that would not be ignored, was I such a wimp when it came to competition work?

In the farmyard, all was quiet. Before going in I went to check on Polly. She greeted me with a friendly whicker, rubbing her black nose up and down my body the way horses do when they are pleased to see you. I gave her some hay and lingered, listening to the comforting sound of munching, trying unsuccessfully to work out a solution to my problems.

Suddenly, from the house the phone started to ring. Hoping it might be news of Gyp, I ran to answer it.

"Tessa?" Mom's voice rang out, anxious and tinged with

relief. "Thank goodness. I've been trying to get in touch with you. You haven't answered my emails."

"Sorry, Mom. It's been a little hectic here lately," I said, without going into details.

"Oh dear. You sound low. Is there anything I can do?"

"Not really. Gyp's missing, among other things." I paused, and then blurted out, "Remember Nick, Dreamcatcher's owner? He wants me to ride in the one-day event he's entered in. Mom, I can't. My insides turn to jelly when I think of all those people watching me."

"Mmm, I know the feeling well," said Mom earnestly.

"What?" I thought I had misheard, and when Mom repeated her words I let out a choked laugh of disbelief. "Come on, Mom! You're famous. You sing in front of those huge audiences. You make it look so easy."

"It's a cultivated art, Tessa. Believe me, I used to be so frozen with stage fright I could hardly speak, never mind sing. An old bandleader friend told me how to master it. You have to breathe deeply and concentrate really hard on something else, preferably whatever is most dear to you. I think about you."

A lump gathered in my throat. All this time, Mom had rated me uppermost in her thoughts and I had not been aware of it.

"It was harder when you were tiny," Mom went on. "But imagining you tucked up safely in bed, Dad there in his study and the babysitter close by in case you awoke, helped to drive away the stage fright gremlins. Eddie was the same, apparently. He thought of Connor."

"Really?"

"Surprised?" Mom gave her throaty chuckle. "Don't be. I can guarantee there's not a public figure who doesn't suffer a degree of nerves when it comes to getting up in front of an audience, and that goes for horse riders too. Once you start riding you'll be fine, I promise. Do you want some breathing exercises that'll help? Have you got a pen handy?"

"Yes," I said.

She reeled them off and had me read them back to make sure I'd written them correctly. "Remember to fix your mind elsewhere. Not on horses, but on a different subject entirely. Maybe the piano. You could try going through a favorite piece of music in your head." She broke off. "Dad always had some Mozart playing in the background when he was at his desk. He said it helped his concentration."

"I remember. Speaking of Dad…" I told her about his phone call. "He sends his regards. He's coming to see me once he gets the okay from the specialist."

"Wonderful! I'm glad he's had that eye problem taken care of. It was bothering him."

A heavy clopping and rumbling in the yard heralded the arrival of Connor. Moments later Bassy's solid shape and a laden log cart went past the window. "Connor's home. I'd better go, Mom."

"All right, darling. Speak to you again soon. I hope the exercises help. Don't forget, find a focus for your thoughts. That's important. 'Bye, Tessa."

The connection ended. Spurred by Mom's suggestion, I wandered into the unused living room, opened the lid of the piano and ran my hands over the keys. It was beautifully in tune. By the time Connor stomped into the house I was well into a soothing Chopin nocturne I knew by heart.

"You're quite some pianist," Connor remarked later as he sat down to tackle some paperwork. Neither of us had

mentioned Gyp. Neither of us looked at the empty basket in the corner.

"Thanks," I replied. "Do you play?"

"No. I had lessons as a kid but I was hopeless. I think Dad decided my talents lay elsewhere. He's self taught, which is amazing. What about your mom?"

"Mom's a trained singer. She went into opera first. Jazz just happens to be her real love." I fiddled with a box of paper clips and said, "I was at the Old Forge today. Things are no better. The horses are still behaving oddly."

"I told you before. You're better off keeping away. I know that village. They'll never accept the Forge being turned into a commercial enterprise. The Meredith pair won't last the year."

"You're wrong," I said hotly. "They like it here. Nick's got his own plans for the place when he finishes school, and there's Lucy. She's talented and ambitious, and she's a really nice person. She deserves to succeed." I paused, pondering. "Connor, do you know the name of the couple that died? The smith who was the start of the trouble?"

"Not that again!" Connor scowled at me across the table. "No, I don't. It's probably been deliberately forgotten along with the true reason for shutting the place down, whatever that might have been."

"Say that again?"

"Well, it could have been anything. A rival smith sets up in business and wants the existing one gone, so he makes up a damaging story. It happens. The same goes on today. People haven't changed all that much."

"You mean you don't believe the smith and his wife met their end in a bad way?"

"Oh, I imagine that much is true. There'd have been

countless accidents with horses in those days, the way there is with modern traffic today. No, it's the superstitious garbage I don't go along with."

"Like horse brass pieces?" I couldn't help myself.

Connor took the dig with good humor. "That's different. Drivers and ploughmen through the years have made their own traditions, and many are based on fatalism and a belief in keeping your luck flowing. I can think of some really tough characters who go along with ancient country lore. There's a shepherd I know who never enters his sheep shed without first touching the doorframe. It's the harmless sort of superstitious quirk that's acceptable. Getting all fired up over some dubious tale of killer horses and bad luck blacksmith's shops is something else."

"There was a spooky feel about the place, Connor. Gyp knew. That's why he ran." I swallowed in remembered fear. "Have you checked in with the police about Gyp? They might have some news."

"I did and they haven't." Connor pushed aside the pile of farming papers. "I can't concentrate on this right now. Maybe I'll have another look for Gyp while it's still light. He's got to be out there somewhere."

"You'd think he'd come home."

"Dogs don't always. I remember Dad losing a sheepdog once. She was living wild up in the hills. He'd just about given up on her when she came back."

"Maybe Gyp will do the same."

"It's a thought. As long as he has access to water and the chance of catching himself a meal, he'll survive. Have you looked in on Polly? I guess I should really call the vet." Connor made a face. "More bills!"

"Stop being so gloomy. Polly's a lot better. I've been

108

treating her with arnica. It's working. Go and see for yourself."

Muttering an unrepeatable comment about old wives' cures under his breath, Connor left, banging his head on the low beam on the way, which did nothing to improve his temper. Through the window I watched him cross the yard and clamber over the stile onto the old lane, and a quiet resolve rose within me. I wasn't giving up on the Merediths and I certainly wasn't giving up on Dreamcatcher. He and I were a team. And now that I had Mom's recipe for mastering those crippling attacks of nerves, I might even consider taking up Nick's challenge.

CHAPTER NINE

I persevered, turning up each day at the Old Forge even though all the camaraderie was now gone. Lucy was quiet and withdrawn. We never had made that visit to the dress shops in town and it looked now as if we never would. A sleek gray kitten took Tishy's place by the kitchen stove.

As for Nick! The change was unbelievable. I thought of the boy with the slanting grin who had made the world look as if it were sprinkled with gold, and longed to be back on our previous happy footing. It was as if the uncanny indomitable force that had affected the animals was at work on the humans too. Had it not been for Dreamcatcher, I might have taken Connor's advice and kept my distance. But Dreamcatcher was coming along splendidly. There were times when he freaked out at nothing and lost concentration, but I could always persuade him back on course, and for now that was enough to keep me focused.

One afternoon Nick said he was getting low on feed and went off in the SUV to the feed store to replenish stocks. I was in the ring, taking Dreamcatcher through the dressage test. It happened unexpectedly. We were approaching the final halt, having executed a credible collected canter across the arena, when all at once the air turned appreciably colder, and from the smithy came the distinct ring of metal on metal.

Dreamcatcher plunged sideways, snatched the bit between his teeth and tore off across the arena, swerving so violently at the bottom rails that I was almost unseated.

"Whoa!" I gasped, groping for a lost stirrup. "Whoa, boy."

He came to a sweating halt and stood staring across at the smithy, his neck arched, muscles as taut as bowstrings, body quivering in alarm. The sound of hammering continued.

Ram, ram, ram!

Puzzled and scared, I patted Dreamcatcher's neck shakily and willed the noise to stop. Then, out of the corner of my eye, I caught sight of a figure standing in the cover of the trees across the field. The sun in my eyes made it impossible to see clearly, but it could have been Annie. She was carrying something. A basket. She'd be out gathering herbs or berries and stopped to look at Dreamcatcher.

Ram, ram, ram!

The noise came again. Darting a panicked glance in that direction, I looked back at the figure in the trees, wondering if she heard it too. The figure did not move and I squinted harder, trying to focus against the splintered rays of sunlight. Despite the heat of the day the coldness was still there around me, chilling my face and bare arms with an icy breath, forming a frost-like barrier that no amount of sunshine could penetrate.

Ram, ram, ram!

"Stop that!" I shrieked, flaring suddenly, shrilly, into anger. "Stop that noise! Go away!"

The hammering ceased abruptly. When I looked again the figure was gone and the warmth was back, scorching and golden. Then came the faintest clamor of hoofbeats and a shouting that could have been canoeists on the river, and then nothing. The silence that followed was profound.

The next instant the cottage door burst open and Lucy emerged. She came sprinting toward the ring.

"Tessa, did you hear ... oh wow, look at Dreamcatcher! He's all worked up!"

"I know. Something spooked him. He's okay now," I said, making a huge effort to pull myself together. No way must Lucy get a hint of what I had just experienced.

"But those noises," Lucy said. "You must have heard them. I was spinning up that batch of dyed wool. It sounded… it was like hammering." She stared at me with enormous eyes that were full of fear. "Tessa, I swear it came from the smithy!"

"It couldn't have," I said as stoutly as I could. "You must be mistaken."

"But I've heard other sounds, too. Like objects being moved around. Scraping sounds. As if someone's in there."

"It could be mice. That place has been shut up for a long time."

"Oh, come on! Since when do mice shift things around?" Lucy said witheringly.

"Maybe it's water pipes. They can make strange noises. Or what you heard could have come from the farm. Sound carries. It may have been the farmer doing some work."

She glanced toward the farmhouse that lay beyond the patch of woodland. "You could be right. He was there yesterday putting up a fence. But…" She darted the smithy another troubled look. "I'll be glad when Nick gets back."

I felt the same but said nothing. Lucy, giving a bewildered little shrug, went back indoors. I gathered up my reins and put Dreamcatcher through some simple track work. It is never a good idea to end a schooling session on a bad note.

All the same, it was a relief to exchange the open ring for the seclusion of Dreamcatcher's stall. Unsaddling, I began to groom him, working slowly and lethargically, every movement an effort after the draining event I had just experienced. Dreamcatcher stood meekly, turning his head now and again to nuzzle my hand for tidbits.

"Good boy," I murmured to him. "You were scared, weren't you? I hope Annie didn't think I was yelling at her – if it was Annie. Still, she'll probably be there on the way back. I can always explain then."

Soon afterwards Nick drove into the yard and I went to help unload the bags of horse feed. We were stacking it in the feed room when a car pulled up on the road and a woman got out. Slim and blonde, she was dressed in a loose fitting navy sport shirt and everyday jodhpurs tucked into form-fitting rubber riding boots.

"Good afternoon," she said briskly. "My name is Jill Hardy. I'm looking for Nick Meredith."

Nick stepped forward. "That's me. How can I help you?"

"I believe you've got my horse." Without wasting any time she ducked back into the car and brought out a photograph, handing it to Nick. "That's Rusty. He was stolen last year from our fields. We tried every way possible to trace him but it was hopeless. He'd simply vanished. It's pure luck that I spotted him today. My son is on the junior canoeing team. I was taking him to the Center and happened to notice Rusty in your ring on the way there. I have his papers at home, if you need extra proof."

Moving to Nick's side, I gazed numbly at the color photo in his hand. There was no debating it. It was Dreamcatcher, all right. At his head stood the woman who was about to bring my fragile world crumbling to dust. Aware of a great hollowness opening up inside me, I waited. I knew, I just knew, what was coming next.

"We had high hopes of Rusty making it as a show jumper. It'll be good to have him back."

Nick, every bit as stunned as I was, cleared his throat noisily. "It never entered my head that he might have been stolen. I picked him up at a sale. He wasn't freeze-branded or identi-chipped. I assumed his owner just wanted to get rid of him."

"Dear me, no! We hadn't had him long when the rustlers took him. I'd meant to get him chipped but time slipped away from me. You know how it is. We have our own yard and buy horses to school and sell; Lowmead. You've probably heard of us."

"Yes," said Nick quietly. The photograph shook slightly in his hand. "Well, what can I say? There's nothing to do but let you take him."

"I'm sorry. This can't be easy for you. Naturally, I'll reimburse any expenses you've had and let you know how Rusty settles."

"Fine," Nick said. "He's a nice horse. Tessa's got him doing very well."

"So I noticed." She swept me a calculated glance of appraisal.

"I suppose you were the person watching us from the trees," I said woodenly.

Her penciled eyebrows shot up. "No. I recognized him from the car. He's quite distinctive. One doesn't get many horses his color. I went on to the canoeing center, dropped my son off and then came straight back here. Our yard isn't too far away. I'll go get the trailer immediately and take Rusty off your hands, okay?"

"Very well," said Nick.

The rest of the afternoon passed in a fog of utter misery. The sparky little roan that had been my dream was gone. He'd be sold by that wretched woman whose sole purpose was to

114

make money off of him. Who knew where he might end up? Nick, his face set, worked off his feelings in a frenzied bout of wood chopping for the stove, while I sat crying in the den, where Lucy plied me with tissues and sympathy.

"I'm so sorry. What you need is something to take your mind off it," Lucy said in desperation. "There's a craft fair in town this week. We were thinking of going. Why not come with us? It'll be a change."

I didn't want a change. I wanted Dreamcatcher back in his stall where he belonged. I shook my head woefully. "Thanks, but I won't. What a horrible woman! Why did she have to go past at that very moment?"

"I'm sorry," Lucy repeated helplessly, hesitating. "I was going to ask if you'd mind looking after things while we're gone like you did before. I suppose now isn't the right time."

"No, that's fine." I blew my nose decisively. "Of course I will."

"Great. Can we make it Saturday? I won't be sorry to get away, to be honest. This place has been getting me down lately."

****

On the way back I looked for Annie, but she was not there and my spirits sank even lower. As I had feared, she must have thought my shouts of reproof were directed at her. People like Annie could be touchy. I hoped she wasn't permanently offended. I had no way of contacting her, no idea where she lived, and no way of clearing the air between us. Thoroughly fed up, I trudged on to Cross Hill.

Connor, when I blurted out what had happened, only grunted and said what else could I expect of a boy of Nick's limited experience. The Gyp scenario still lay heavily between us. The long, unrewarding hours of searching had dwindled. Connor took out his grief and frustration in the forest, fiendishly clearing the thickets of unwanted growth, coming home exhausted and irritable. Today he was more silent than ever and I made my escape to the front room and the piano.

Until, wonderfully, Dad called.

"Chin up," he said, after I had poured out my woes. Dad always said that. Chin up, whenever I'd fallen off a pony. Chin up if I didn't get the expected grades at school… chin up when he told me he and Mom were separating. "In fact, Tessa, I've called with some news."

It turned out he'd been given the all clear from his specialist and was now looking forward to coming back home and resuming work. "There's a new geological survey I'm interested in. But I can explain when I see you."

"When will that be?" I asked him breathlessly.

"Not immediately. There are a number of things to sort out first. Tessa, about that other matter we spoke of."

"The Old Forge?"

"Yes. I've been thinking. Why not take another look around? You may come across some clue that would throw some light on the mystery."

"But it's still boarded up. I haven't said anything to the others. They still don't know I went in there."

"I see," he said, mildly. "All the same, it might be worth a try."

Recalling the strange hammering that had issued from the shuttered blackness of the smithy, the chilling whispers at night, my grip tightened on the phone. *Devil Horse! Devil Horse!* It had all started after I had entered the place. What might repeating the process stir up? But

116

then I thought of Dad waiting patiently on the line; his eager intellect, the crystal-clear way he had of assessing a situation. Dad was no fool. If he made a suggestion it was a valid one.

"I'll think about it," I said.

"Great. Let me know how it goes. 'Bye, Tessa."

I was halfway through a Mozart piece when it hit me that on Saturday I would have the Old Forge to myself, and my hands came to a stop on the keys. Here was my chance to carry out Dad's suggestion – providing I could find the courage! I kept on playing, but my stomach already churned and the uplifting cadences no longer had any effect. And later when I went to bed, the nightmare returned, as dark and scary as ever. The rattle and clatter of a horse and buggy. The hateful whispering.

Devil horse!

CHAPTER TEN

Polly was recovered now and back at work, leaving Bassy free to help me spend the next days combing the woods for Annie. She must have been sulking, because she did not show up. By the time Saturday arrived I was at such a fever pitch I'd almost decided not to follow through with Dad's scheme.

After Nick and Lucy left, however, I fed the gray kitten and went out, shutting the door behind me. It had gotten very dark. Thunder muttered in the distance as I collected the tools from the garden shed.

Not long afterwards I was entering the smothering blackness of the smithy, my insides lurching at every small sound. With every step, dust from the dried heaps of moldering manure on the floor rose in choking clouds. A dead rat by the workbench, and another close to the anvil, brought a start of surprise. Rats and mice, as a rule, expired in the seclusion of their holes and not in the open.

Other than the small grim corpses, everything looked the same. There was the furnace, the anvil and other gear. On the cobwebby shelf above the workbench were some official-looking tin boxes. Taking one down, I shook off the decades of vermin droppings and dust and levered off the lid. It held a set of hard-backed books, each labeled with the year – the blacksmith's ledgers of accounts, by the look of it.

Beyond the entrance, the summer storm moved closer.

In a bright flash of lightning, I glimpsed the year of entry on the front of the one I held. 1901.

Over a hundred years had passed since the record had been made. Taking it to the doorway where the light was better, I opened it. The tin box had kept the book in remarkably good shape, for though the pages were yellowed with age, the writing in faded, black ink was legible. The smith had named not only his clients but their horses or ponies too. Beside each animal was a memo noting any quirks of behavior or recurring hoof problems.

"Miller Tarrant's Violet," I read aloud. "Piebald cob. Set of working shoes with studs. Fidget. Heat in off-fore. Soft feet." And, "Mr. Darcy Wright's Lancer. Gray Thoroughbred. Set of lightweight shoes. Nice mannered. Good solid feet."

On the very bottom line was entered a horse called Wishful. It was a pretty name, and clearly the smith had a special fondness for the animal, since he had written, "Farmer Dale's Wishful. Bay-brown carriage horse. Elderly. Set of medium shoes. A good sort." And in brackets, a poignant reminder. (Likes apples. Must get him one from orchard.)

Eagerly I turned the page, only to find it and every successive one afterwards blank. Going through the book again, I found a pattern to the shoeing appointments. Due to the poor quality of her hooves, the miller's mare Violet required more attention than Mr. Wright's sounder Lancer. Wishful's name cropped up with a staunch regularity, accompanied by some tender missive that brought a catch to the throat.

"Ate up his treat with relish and enjoyed a carrot for a change."

The very last entry was for Wishful and this, I noticed, had not been checked off as all the others had. It was as if the smith had been unexpectedly called out and not completed his paperwork for the day. Or perhaps something else had happened. Something far more devastating and final.

The page was dated the 21st of August – today's date!

A crash of thunder heralded the first smattering of rain that quickly became a deluge and drove me back into the heart of the smithy. Returning the book to the box, I stood pondering what I had discovered.

If the smith truly had met his end through a vicious horse as believed, then why did the facts not compute? The very last horse to come under the smith's hands was a good-natured tractable sort, a favorite that the owner liked and respected. Any horse person knows that accidents can happen with even the quietest animals – Lucy's childhood experience was proof of that. This was a man who had spent his entire life with horses and ponies. He knew them. If any had been about to misbehave, he would have been ready for it.

Around and around went my thoughts, trying to make sense out of the situation, an equation that did not add up. Here was a biddable horse, not strange to the place, and not ill at ease in any way. He was standing quietly while the smith removed the old worn shoes, pared back the overgrown hoof and began the skilled task of fitting the new set. I could picture it: the roaring red furnace, the air thick with smoke and the acrid stench of hot metal and burning hoof. Customer and smith were engaged in a little light banter as one held the horse and the other labored. The horse was wishful, innocent and trusting, turning his head in polite interest as Dreamcatcher had done, wanting his juicy treat.

As before when I stood here, time started to shift. The rowdy beating of rain on the roof receded and the coldness was there, chasing away the turgid heat of the day. Before my eyes the empty furnace took on a rosy glow. Shapes emerged, forming a horse, his bay coat burnished by the light of the flames, obediently lifting a fore hoof at the bidding of the smith, while the owner stood at his head. All at once the smith paused and clutched at his chest, his face contorting as if with pain. After a moment or two he continued working, murmuring soothingly to the horse as he did so.

Hardly daring to breathe, I watched him, wanting to see more. But then there was an enormous clap of thunder overhead and the scene immediately began to fragment in front of me. My eyes were gritty with dust and I blinked, rubbing them, and when I focused again the scene was gone. I was back in the smothering dimness of the abandoned blacksmith's shop, with the furnace dead and cheerless, the drumming of rain above and the hiss and splatter of it on the road outside.

A soft mewling and something brushing my legs caused me to look down, and there, unbelievably, was Tishy. She was a little thinner perhaps, her fluffy coat unkempt, but it was Tishy all the same, alive and well and purring fit to burst.

"Tishy!" I scooped her up in my arms. "Where have you been? Wait till Lucy sees you. Who's been clearing out those pesky rats? Clever kitty."

Moving the cat to the kitchen for safekeeping, I left her warily acquainting herself with the new kitten and ducked back through the downpour for another look around. The box of account books lay on the bench top where I had left it. Wedged down the side of the tin was another slim volume I

had missed earlier. Heart quickening, I held it up in the dim light to make out the name written on the cover.

Dan Shone. His Journal.

Dan *Shone*? Did that mean what I thought, that Annie who had appeared to me in Black Woods was the blacksmith's wife? Arms covered with goose bumps, I opened the book and began to read. The writing was smudged and faded, but I had the gist of it. Dan, muscled and strong, had suffered "spasms of the heart that leave me gasping for breath and gripping my chest in agony. Lately the attacks have worsened and I fear this will be the end of me. My Annie must not know, for she will only worry."

So that was it. I recalled how, in that brief glimpse into the past, the smith had stopped and clutched his chest, and now I knew why. Blacksmith Dan Shone had not been killed by the horse at all. His untimely death was due to a crippling heart attack that had proved fatal. What had happened wasn't difficult to work out. Dan falling under the horse as the pain overtook him. Wishful, startled, pulling back, jerking the rope from his owner's hand, perhaps rearing, doing his utmost to avoid the inert form on the floor as those thrashing fore-hooves came down again. Annie springing to the rescue, the horse alarmed and making for the open door, oblivious in its panic and confusion to her slight figure. The glancing blow. The crack of bone against stone. Then silence, into which came the roar of the untended furnace.

"Oh, Annie, you've been so wrong all this time," I cried. "Wishful was innocent, and here's the proof of it."

A slight sound in the doorway made me glance up – and there she was.

"Annie?" I said in a scared voice. She wasn't real. It was

a phantom I saw and yet here she was, the Annie I knew in her shabby brown dress, hair all over the place and eyes bright and knowing.

"Hello, Tessa." She came into the smithy, glancing around. "It hasn't changed at all. What was it you said about Wishful?"

She didn't seem threatening in any way and my fears disappeared. I said, calmly and matter-of-factly, "Wishful didn't kill your husband, Annie. Dan was very ill."

"Ill? My Dan? Rubbish! He was strong and fit. The horse turned on him."

"No he didn't. Dan died of a heart attack. Here, read this." I pushed the journal into her hands. "These are Dan's own words."

Annie's face saddened at the sight of Dan's large clumsy handwriting, then crumpled as she took in what it said. "It's coming back to me," she whispered, looking up. "Dan did grip his chest just before the commotion started. He often did. Indigestion, he said it was. I never thought to question him. Well, he was a vigorous man. He'd never ailed in his life till then."

"I'm sorry, Annie. It was a terrible thing to happen. The horse wasn't to blame, though. Wishful went into a panic when Dan collapsed with the heart attack, but he didn't kill Dan."

"No. I see that now." Annie sighed heavily. "I've been wrong to keep the animal's spirit imprisoned here, haven't I? All this time, and it wasn't his fault."

"Annie, what happened to Wishful after he took fright and ran out?"

"He escaped into the hills and lived wild there. I couldn't rest until I'd gotten my revenge. He was an old

124

horse, so I waited for him to meet his natural end and then I kept his spirit confined so he couldn't have peace. Have you seen the charms on the door?"

"The paws and snouts? Oh, Annie!"

"It was a good spell. It held him fast, until you came along, wanting to put things right…" Her voice was fading, becoming part of the air currents and the distant rush of the river.

"But the hoof and wheel prints, Annie," I pressed. "How could Wishful have made those if he was shut in here? It isn't possible."

"Anything's possible once you've crossed the stream," Annie said. "He'd have sent those tracks in desperation. He'd have wanted someone to find them and help him. Poor Wishful. I'll have to beg his forgiveness, won't I?"

Her gaze moved beyond the anvil, and following it I saw the faint outline of the sturdy bay carriage horse, and felt the atmosphere in the smithy subtly change, as if Annie's plea was acknowledged. Whether it was accepted I could not tell, and when I looked back, Annie was gone.

With a strange feeling of loss, I wondered if I would see her again, and why she had appeared to me in the first place. I hadn't been exactly happy at the time and neither had she.

Leaving everything as it was, I returned to the cottage to wait for Nick and Lucy.

The lightning storm was over by the time they arrived. Seeing the opened building and the telltale heap of planking outside, they came charging into the cottage at hyper speed.

"Tessa, what in –" Lucy stopped, her gaze falling on her missing cat who came dancing up on velvet paws to greet her. "Tishy! Oh, Tishy!"

125

While Lucy fussed over her pet, Nick asked what had been going on. "It's a long story," I said. "It might be best for you to come and see for yourselves."

Outside, a strengthening sun drew the moisture from the road in steaming clouds. Lucy paled when she saw the tiny mummified remains on the scuffed old door. "Ugh! What are those?"

"Nothing much. They're harmless."

It was the truth. The power of the charm was long used up.

In the smithy I showed them the account books and Dan Shone's journal. For some reason I had never mentioned Annie to Lucy or even Nick. She had just been someone I chatted to on journeys along the old lane, a countrywoman with an astonishing affinity with the natural world. Now, I hugged the memory of those encounters to myself, a secret to revere in years to come.

We've got to help each other out, haven't we, Tessa?

She had certainly helped me. I felt privileged to have known Annie and would always be grateful to her for passing on her knowledge of plants and their properties.

"So what made you come barging in here when nobody else would?" Nick enquired.

"Oh, reasons. I hated the thought of a horse being branded a killer. No horse is that. Wishful certainly wasn't. I think if you were to spread the findings around the village it would alter people's attitude a lot."

"Maybe." Lucy sounded dubious.

"Tessa could be right, Lucy," said Nick. He took a more serious look around him and gave a sharp intake of breath. "There are possibilities here for more than just a straightforward shop. This could be fixed up as a working museum-cum-shop. Think what a tourist attraction that would be."

"Well, yes…" Lucy, still shaken by the turn of events, caught sight of Tishy's long-tailed trophies on the floor. If anything she went a shade whiter. "Ugh! That accounts for the scratching sounds I heard. But… how come Tishy was here in the first place?"

"She must have come in after the vermin." Nick pointed to a rat-nibbled gap at the foot of the door. "She could easily have squeezed through there. It's weird she never did it before, though."

"Well, actually, this wasn't my first time here," I confessed in a voice that wobbled. "Tishy must have gotten on the rats' trails then. She must have hung around till they were all taken care of."

"You mean…?" Lucy stared at me, realization dawning. "The day we went to the accountants! That's when all the trouble started. Oh, Tessa, how could you?"

"I'm so sorry," I said unhappily. "I didn't know then what had happened here or I wouldn't have done it. I wanted to find out why people were so hostile toward you. The smithy seemed a good place to start."

"I think Tessa made the right move," Nick said. "What an odd thing. This funny business with the horses had really gotten to me. I was on edge all the time. I'm fine now, though. How about you, Lucy?"

"I'm not sure." Lucy needed some convincing.

"Oh, come on. Tessa's done us a big favor here. Opening the place up was what it needed. What happened here was tragic, but it wasn't evil. People just thought it was and that's what gave The Old Forge its bad name."

"It gave me nightmares," I said.

"Really?" Nick sent me a hint of his old quirky grin. "Do you have any more surprises in store?"

"Isn't this enough for one day?" I countered.

I spoke too soon, for a car drew up outside. A door slammed. Moments later a shadow fell across the entrance and a brisk voice called out, "Hello? Is anybody there? Ah, here you are. I wonder if I might have a word?"

CHAPTER ELEVEN

Into the smithy came Jill Hardy.

"What an extraordinary place," she said, glancing around. "Actually, I've come about Rusty. I promised to let you know how he was doing."

Lucy stared. I glowered. "And?" Nick said.

"Not very well, I'm afraid. The move hasn't done him any good at all. He just isn't settling. Rusty never was the easiest of rides but now he's impossible. He dumped my husband, and the girl who helps us did no better."

"Huh," said Nick. "I'm sorry to hear that, but I'm not surprised. He was very happy here with us. I'd even considered entering him for the one-day event next weekend. I'd still go for it, given the chance."

Jill Hardy said, "The Rydale One-Day Event? It's rather advanced for Rusty, I'd say, especially now that the move's unsettled him."

"He'd be fine for me," I blurted out, and then had to wonder. Riding schools differ in their schooling methods. A patient approach was not much in evidence here. What if Dreamcatcher was unrideable? The thought only made me more determined. "I know he would."

"Oh, really?" The pink-glossed lips tweaked frostily. "You sound very sure."

"I am sure. We get along very well. We always have."

"Good heavens, what an ego!"

Jill Hardy obviously thought I was boasting, but I didn't

care because what I said was the truth. She looked pensive, as if collecting her thoughts. Then, "Okay," she said. "If that's how you feel, how would you like Rusty back?"

Lucy opened her mouth to speak and shut it again. I simply gaped. Nick said indignantly, "What do you mean, if that's how Tessa feels? Of course the horse would go well for her. She's an ace rider."

"In that case you won't have a problem," Jill Hardy said, now goaded beyond endurance. "I'll make a deal with you. If Tessa rides in the event and wins, the horse is yours for the sum I paid you. Otherwise he's mine to do whatever I please with. I'll probably sell him. We're overstocked at the moment. My husband was at a sale the day I found Rusty and went a little overboard. We've got more horses than we seriously need, so one less would be no bad thing." She paused. "Well?"

There was an agonizing moment of suspense as Nick hesitated. Lucy said surprisingly, "Oh, go on, Nick. You know you like the horse."

"It's really up to Tessa," Nick said. "She's the one who'll be riding him."

Three pairs of eyes turned gruelingly on me. Pity shone in the deep blue of Lucy's. Nick's wore a gleam of open challenge. Jill Hardy's narrowed. "Well?"

My throat was dry. I swallowed hard and heard myself say, "Okay, but could we enter him as Dreamcatcher and not Rusty?"

"I don't see why not," Jill Hardy said.

* * * *

Before the day was over, Dreamcatcher was back at the Old Forge; a very disturbed Dreamcatcher, wild-eyed, sweaty, and ready with a maiming kick for anyone who tried to get too close. To regain his shattered trust I spent the entire evening with him in his stall, earning myself a scolding from Connor for being late back.

"But Lucy said she'd called to explain," I protested.

"She also made a point of letting me know when you started back. Does it always take Bassy the better part of an hour to get up the lane?"

I said nothing. The truth was I had lingered in Black Woods in the rash hope of seeing Annie. She had not come. The little woods remained airy and silent in the gathering twilight. Yearningly I searched the shadows, willing her to appear, wanting to come across her among the trees. If she was there she did not show herself. It was as if she had completed her part in the scheme of things and now it was up to me. I knew I had to focus on Dreamcatcher and the coming event.

Later, I emailed Mom the news and called Dad.

"Best of luck," Dad said quietly. He must have wondered about my unexpected change of heart for competition, but being Dad he did not question it.

That night I slept soundly. Cantering through my dreams went my willing little roan with the heart of a lion. There was no menacing pounding of hooves or jangle of carriage wheels. No whispering to shake the peace. I woke to the misty light of a new day and a wonderful sense of purpose. Dreamcatcher was back. I just had to master my inhibitions and he could be back for good.

****

At the Old Forge the pile of unwanted boards had been cleared away, and the neglected outside walls washed down. The unloved building was looking as if someone cared at last.

"Dreamcatcher's up," greeted Nick. "I turned him out

in his paddock after you left last night. He always was happiest out there."

"Was he quiet?"

"He did some tearing around, but nothing much. Do you want to go for a trail ride? Or are you just going to concentrate on schooling for the next seven days?"

"Six," I corrected. "Only six to go – wow! Nick, are you going ahead with the competition?"

"What do you think?" Nick said with a grin. He looked at me closely. "Tessa, about Dreamcatcher. If you get lucky at the event he's yours for keeps."

I stared, breathless, disbelieving. "You mean it?"

"Yes, I do. Dreamcatcher's been yours from the start. You don't have to worry about where to keep him. He can stay here as a lease. There are school vacations. I can't see you staying in the city when there's Cross Hill to come to, can you?"

For a reply I flung my arms around Nick's neck and hugged him.

I'll never know where the next week went. Every moment of every day was spent with Dreamcatcher, trail riding and schooling in the dressage arena and the jumping paddock. It wasn't until Thursday that I dared risk the cross-country. We still had not reached our previous comfort level, but Dreamcatcher tucked in his chin and took the course boldly. I refused to contemplate the fast-approaching weekend and my first ever ride under the searing gaze of the public.

With Nick also working all-out toward the event, it was left up to Lucy to spread the word about Dan Shone and his journal. Riding through the village, I noticed a heartening change of attitude, an unbending. People now acknowledged us with nods and smiles. At the General Store – the worst offender for casting doubt over the Meredith venture – the owner shamelessly inquired if Lucy was interested in her father's woodcuts for the upcoming shop.

"Certainly," Lucy said, and came back beaming.

At the pharmacy the young assistant mentioned a party of hikers who had spotted a stray dog up in the hills. Lucy called the farm immediately. Hardly daring to hope, Connor renewed his search for Gyp.

On the evening before the event I gave Dreamcatcher's tack the cleaning of its life and groomed him until his mottled coat took on the gleam of molten metal. Presentation mattered. I wanted him spruced up with the best of them and spent a long time tidying his mane and tail. Lastly I picked out his newly shod hooves, and then stood back to judge how he might compare with the classy animals he would be up against the next day.

"Stop worrying," ordered Nick from the door. "He looks great."

* * * *

The first light saw me braiding Dreamcatcher. In the next stall, Nick was similarly occupied with Rough Tweed. Sea Holly, ready and waiting in travel rug and boots, announced the arrival of the hired trailer with a loud whinny. We loaded the horses and Lucy, who was following later in the car, came out to wave goodbye.

On the short journey to the big dairy farm where the event was held, Nick drilled me on everything: form, the briefing, walking the courses, riding in, the first horse inspection, and that all-important timing for cross-country. At the back of my mind, Mom's mantra for calmness ticked away soothingly.

"Here we are," Nick said as the trailer turned into a narrow lane with deep ditches on either side, and then onto a field where two officials pointed us alongside a tall hedge.

It was a popular event, with generous prize money and a friendly atmosphere. The main drawback was the trail, which, due to the hilly terrain, looked tough on the horses. It looked tough on the riders too if they were unfortunate enough to take a spill. With a pang I glanced at the first aid van and looked quickly away again.

The parking lot was already filling up with trucks and trailers. On the steps of a nearby vehicle, a small boy sat solemnly chomping his way through a sandwich.

"We have lots of time." Nick was calm, and I envied him. "Let's check on the horses."

Dreamcatcher had sweated a little during the journey, but then so had Sea Holly. I chalked it up to them being stalled next to each other – which was a mistake, since Dreamcatcher had probably spent the entire trip getting her wound up with his awful faces. Other than that, he seemed to be taking everything in stride.

Nick went off to get our numbers from the secretary's "tent," a trailer in the corner of the field adjacent to the farmyard, and others began to follow in his wake. My number was fifteen. I had a fifteenth birthday coming up soon.

"I hope this is lucky," I said, pinning it on.

All around us, the parking lot was coming to life. People were unloading horses, and tethering them to groom and saddle up. A couple of black Labradors bounded along the hedgerow, stopping now and then to sniff rabbit scents. Somewhere a terrier yapped excitedly. From the depths of a truck a horse whinnied. Another answered and this set up a chorus along the line of vehicles.

"Stop that!" Nick yelled to Rough Tweed, who insisted on accompanying his neighs with an energetic battering on the side of the trailer.

By nine o'clock the field swarmed with activity. A group of farmers, enlisted as jump stewards, took up their positions with clipboards in hand.

The breeze picked up, chasing a few ominous little clouds across the sun.

"I told you it could rain," Nick remarked gloomily as we went to walk the course set out over several hillocky fields and stretches of sparse woodland. As far as Nick could see the first real problem came at fence six, a tall brush with an open ditch in front. This was followed by a choice of a gentle turn on several strides around a tree to a smaller brush, or a bolder angle going under the tree.

"I'm opting for the first," Nick said. "You might get away with the second choice on Dreamcatcher. He's supple enough. It'll save you time, too."

Another possible hitch was the water jump, which had a choice of routes, neither of which looked like time savers. Nick thought the right-hand approach looked best for his lankier horses. It would definitely be the left choice for us, I decided with growing confidence. The rest of the course seemed straightforward, with terrific gallops across open country where points could be gained.

Time was passing so we hurried back to the trailer. One or two latecomers appeared, bumping over the uneven field in search of a parking space. One girl, having ridden here, complained that a tractor had overtaken her and splashed them with mud.

"That's how it goes!" said Nick good-naturedly, handing the girl a bucket with some of our precious water for a quick cleanup.

The loudspeaker came on with a shriek that made everyone

look up and got the terrier barking again. Competitors were called for the briefing, in which the day's proceedings were outlined. After that came the first horse inspection, where the horses were trotted out in front of the judges to show their paces and condition. When the event was over they would undergo a second inspection, proving them sound competition animals or otherwise.

Spectators were gathered around the dressage arena now, sitting on straw bales put there for that purpose or on portable seats they had brought with them.

"We'd better mount up," Nick said, spurring me to put Mom's breathing exercises into operation. Like a mantra, I chanted, *In through the nose and out again. In through the nose and out. Think Mozart. Think Chopin. Think Rachmaninov.* Nothing could beat that second concerto for gaining concentration…

Sea Holly was Nick's first ride, with Tweed following later. Nick looked amazingly attractive and somehow remote in his pristine white jodhpurs, gleaming black boots, black jacket with tails and snowy white shirt. Watching him ride off to the exercise area for some warming up, I felt suddenly like a novice and completely inadequate. I had lost weight over the summer and my cream-colored jodhpurs and dark blue jacket, the only decent outfit I had with me, felt loose. I wished I had long hair that could be tucked elegantly into a hairnet like some of the other competitors, instead of sticking out stubble-like under my hat. Dreamcatcher too looked out of place among the warmbloods and Thoroughbreds, with their good solid colors and muscled grace. Then again, he had a presence that attracted attention.

"I like your horse," said a cheerful girl on a leggy bay. "I bet he's a character."

136

"Yes, he is," I replied, running my hand over Dreamcatcher's taut neck. Breathing therapy was fine for me, but what about him? I could only hope that my calmness would communicate down the reins.

"He looks powerful. I bet you've had to train him gently."

"Well, sort of." I swallowed, thinking of the concentrated schooling, the long hours of confidence gaining, and the panic that he would not be ready in time. Beside us, the bay stood chomping his bit in deep concentration. He reminded me of a kindly uncle, the sort that spoils you rotten and doesn't mind when you play pop music at full blast. "Your horse is terrific too," I said.

"Oh yes... but then I'm prejudiced." Slapping her mount's shoulder affectionately, the girl nodded toward a boy on a tall black horse and said in a low voice, "There's Pete Marsh on Rocky Road. Watch his test. They're perfect."

Some of the competitors on super-fit mounts were members of the local eventing squad, and laughed and joked together as they waited their turn. One boy, who had won a previous event with his 16.1-hand gray, got a lot of well-intentioned ribbing.

"What are you doing here, Jake? Did you forget you qualified?"

"Probably just living up to his horse's name."

The girl on the bay giggled. Jake's horse was named Doubly Sure.

A call came for quiet and the dressage began. The boy on the black did a beautifully balanced test that won him high marks from the judges.

"See what I mean?" whispered the girl on the bay.

Next, looking relaxed and mentally prepared, went the squad member on the gray. They gave a customary polished performance but left the arena with several points less than the Rocky Road combination. Nick and Sea Holly followed. Sea Holly really looked great, and squeezed between the previous two into second place. A few riders later, Nick placed Rough Tweed fractionally behind Holly, to his delight.

The girl on the bay botched the halt, had the transitions totally wrong and came out rueful. "It's my fault. I should have ridden him in instead of watching the others. Oh well, better luck in the cross-country."

Everything felt strangely unreal, as if I were another person and not Tessa Darcy at all. Our number was called and into the arena we went.

Breathe, Tessa. In, out. In, out.

Dreamcatcher was tenser than he was at home, but he seemed happy to be here and that gave me the boost I needed. However, my stupid nerves still got the better of me as we came down the center line and halted beautifully – but at Y instead of H! Furious at myself, since I couldn't afford to throw marks away so stupidly, I made a concentrated effort and completed the test without another hitch, placing us between Rough Tweed and the squad rider on the gray.

"Tough luck," Nick said when I came out of the arena with scorching cheeks. "Don't let it get to you. Anyone can make mistakes."

Gritting my teeth, I resolved that there would be no more.

In the cross-country, Nick made a fantastic round on Tweed but fell behind with Holly. That dubious fence number six was responsible for many changes in the leaderboard and we saw the boy on the gray and my new friend on the bay drop out of contention.

139

Dreamcatcher, to my utter elation, flew over the course. He caused me an anxious moment when I risked the shortcut to the small brush, faltering, but regained his balance cleverly and took the jump with catlike ease, galloping on, his head down and tail pluming. As if in a dream I heard the scattered applause and pressed on, leaving it mostly to Dreamcatcher who was now into his stride.

"Oh, good job!" shouted Nick as we galloped past the finish, mud-splattered, lathered and panting.

"It wasn't me," I gasped, "it was Dreamcatcher."

"I bet it got you to third place." Nick strained in the saddle, avidly watching the numbers change on the board. "It has! Oh, great!"

The three top spots now stood with Pete Marsh on Rocky Road in the lead, then Rough Tweed a close second and third Dreamcatcher. Somewhere among the spectators, Jill Hardy watched. I pictured the wry set of her mouth and wondered if she was having regrets about her decision to let Dreamcatcher go.

"Have you seen Lucy?" Nick enquired as we rode back to the trailer to clean the horses and rest them before the jumping.

"No." I'd been too focused on what I was doing to give her a thought. "She could be watching from the trees. Connor should be here somewhere too."

"Oh, good." He leaned across and gave Dreamcatcher a resounding slap on the neck. "Good boy. What a great show you put up, the two of you. You're soul mates. You belong together."

I said nothing. Everything now depended on the show jumping.

We took care of the horses, gulped down some bottled water, and brushed the now dried mud from our clothes. Nick, who had brought a change of clothes, got into his jumping gear in the trailer. The rain that had threatened earlier had not materialized and the day had turned out fine and warm. It was early evening now, the sun starting to sink behind the hills in fiery streaks. In the exercise ring, competitors were putting their mounts over the practice jump.

"Do you want to give it a try?" asked Nick, sliding a saddle on Sea Holly.

I shook my head. "Maybe later. You go ahead. I'm exhausted. What I'd give for some chocolate."

"Try the cooler," Nick said.

Looking inside, I discovered alongside the other food enough chocolate bars to supply half the showground, thoughtfully provided by Lucy! Nick put Sea Holly over the practice fence, after which we joined the other competitors in the jumping ring to walk the course.

The obstacles were arranged in a traditional figure-eight. The worst hazard was the big combination fence set at an awkward angle – it would be very hard for Tweed with his great lumbering stride, jarring for Holly who liked to know precisely what was in front of her. And Dreamcatcher? For the first time that day, I quailed. Not because of the course itself, which he was athletic enough to cope with, but at the brilliantly-hued tubs of flowers at the foot of some of the jumps; a spectacular blaze of color guaranteed to provoke the spooking attack of the century!

As we were leaving the ring, I caught sight of a bright golden head in the crowd that stopped me in my tracks.

"Mom!" I yelped. "There's Mom! Oh, wow!"

Eddie stood beside her, grinning broadly.

"Darling!" cried Mom, ducking under the ropes and rushing up to envelope me in a perfumed hug. "Thank

141

goodness we got here at last. We've just seen the leader-board. Tessa, you're in third place!"

"Not bad, huh?" added Eddie. "Hi, Tessa. How're things?"

"Ask me again later," I said shakily, making the introductions. Nick asked if they had stopped first at Cross Hill.

"I wasn't allowed." Eddie sent a telling nod toward Mom. "We hot-footed it from the airport. The flight was delayed, or we'd have been here for the start."

"I was panicking. I thought we'd never make it," Mom said. "Still, we saw the cross-country. Third place! How wonderful! You looked so confident, Tessa!"

"Thanks to Rachmaninov," I told her, bringing puzzled looks from Eddie and Nick.

We exchanged a glance of pure understanding, and Mom smiled her famous smile. "Is Connor here? I was sure he would be."

"I don't know," I said. "We haven't seen Lucy yet either. The place is very spread out. They could be anywhere."

The loudspeaker system crackled a warning. Nick said we had to go. "Fingers crossed for us!" I called over my shoulder as he hustled me away, then laughed when Mom and Eddie each raised a hand and did just that.

All my hopes hung on the show jumping. One false move, and Dreamcatcher was lost to me forever.

CHAPTER TWELVE

The show jumping was intense, with many riders washing out at the combination. It was surprising for Pete Marsh and Rocky Road that after a leading dressage score and an impressive cross-country round, they picked up eight penalties in the jumping ring. Pete was a terrific sport and left the ring laughing and slapping his horse's neck affectionately.

"Good old Rocky! He enjoyed today! He thinks it's all one big party!"

Not all the competitors had the same attitude. I was entering the collecting ring on Dreamcatcher, striving for inner calm, when along came a woman I had noticed earlier. She had been unfortunate at the start of the cross-country, when she had parted company from her racy chestnut at the second fence and withdrawn.

She looked Dreamcatcher over, lip curling. "Peculiar color, isn't he? Not the best head either. I never go for a horse with a dished face, myself. I always find it's a sign of poor concentration."

My friend with the bay was quick. "Really?" she said, sugar-sweet. "I thought it was a mark of intelligence. You get it in all the Arab lines, don't you? I don't think you can get much brainier than that."

Casting us a glower fit to scorch the grass beneath our feet, the woman stalked off.

"Witch!" muttered the girl, who like many others had

flipped at the combination and had now put her bay in its stall to come and view the rest. "Pay no attention. Good luck with the jumping."

"Thanks." I watched her move off and find a place at ringside, then dismounted to check Dreamcatcher's bridle. "You mustn't spook," I told him. "The flowers are not going to leap out and mug you. I promise."

Dreamcatcher gave a breathy nicker and butted me in the chest for mints. "Not yet. Afterwards. We've got to do our very best."

Remounting, I rode into the collecting ring in time to see Nick jump a clear round on Tweed. Sea Holly had also gone clear and so had a number of other competitors, altering the leader-board confusingly.

Nick left the ring to loud applause. He was grinning and thumping Tweed's neck with delight.

"Nick, that was terrific!" I said. "You've got a chance."

"Let's wait and see." He glanced up as the loudspeaker boomed out my number and said rapidly, "You'll have to go clear and neat. Watch that combination. It's a killer. Good luck."

Taking the deepest breath ever, I pressed my legs into Dreamcatcher's sides and urged him into the ring accompanied by the announcement over the loudspeaker.

"And now we have number fifteen. Tessa Darcy riding Mrs. Jill Hardy's Dreamcatcher."

Of his own accord Dreamcatcher broke into a bouncy canter, fly bucking, showing off, tucking in his chin and bringing up his hooves delicately. The crowd loved it, bursting into ripples of laughter. Just in time I remembered to make my acknowledgement to the judge, bowing in the saddle as gracefully as I could under the circumstances. I caught a glimpse of Mom's white face and Eddie's fixed smile. Then the starting bell rang. Shortening my reins, I sat tight and said, "Come on, Dreamcatcher! Let's go for it!"

He responded like the showman he was. We took the first poles and the small wall nimbly and careered around the first bend to jump the stile and a jazzy double in the same manner. Turning recklessly, we crossed the ring at a sharp canter, heading for the combination and its startling array of potted plants.

"Steady," I said, sitting up in the saddle to take my weight off Dreamcatcher's back, not interfering with his mouth but letting him know I meant business. "Careful. No balking. Go on!"

Letting out a snort of utter horror at the dazzle of scarlet geraniums and bright-yellow daisies, he flexed his jaw, gathered himself and soared over the awkward assembly of poles with an ease that brought a gasp from ringside and had me clinging on by his braids. A round of applause sent him flicking his ears in appreciation, but did not stop him from giving his fans what they wanted. Dreamcatcher tore on, terribly out of control, taking the water jump, the brush and the final set of simple poles with a triumphant flourish of his heels as if to say, "there you go, everyone! Beat that if you can!"

"And she's done it!" roared the man behind the loudspeaker. "She's clear! Well done, Tessa Darcy on Dreamcatcher!"

Managing to pull up at the exit, I looked down at Nick's ecstatic face. "You made it! Wow – what a round!"

"It wasn't me. I just pointed him in the right direction. Where are the mints? He deserves the whole pack!"

So far, so good. Now we had a jump-off against the clock to face.

Only four other horses including Rough Tweed and Sea Holly had gone clear. The wait for the jumps to be raised and the course reorganized seem to go on forever. Across the ring, Mom sent me a thumbs-up sign. Beside her, Eddie pointed.

"Look," I whispered to Nick. "Over there by my folks. It's Lucy and Connor."

And between them, securely held on a length of rope, was Gyp!

There was no time for explanations. The order came to mount up and Nick was called into the ring. This time Sea Holly came unstuck at the raised combination and was out of the running. The same went for the next rider, but Tweed made a clear if careful round, not pulling any punches as far as speed went. Feeling a tremor due more to excitement than nerves, I leaned forward and whispered endearments in Dreamcatcher's ear.

"Good boy. Clever little horse. Let's do our best, okay?"

The fourth horse was careless at the wall and dislodged a brick but made good time. Our number was called. We entered the ring with Dreamcatcher playing to the crowd as before, bringing spontaneous applause and some delighted hoots.

The bell rang. Gathering my reins and my wits, I fixed my gaze between Dreamcatcher's ears and took him in a wide circle. "Come on. This is it!"

Dreamcatcher didn't need to be told twice. Dropping his head, he launched himself at the first jump, clearing it easily, throwing himself at the second, and going all-out to make up speed. So fast was his pace that he skidded violently on the turn in a way that would have brought a bigger horse down, but not my little roan. We hopped over the raised wall and made another skidding turn for the straight run across the ring and that difficult triple. Collecting him, I felt his fly buck of objection at the restriction on his mouth, heard the nervous titter of the onlookers, and was aware of the collectively held breath as I let him go. The blaze of flowers shot by us in a blur and Dreamcatcher jumped, clearing the first, putting in two clever strides where the bigger horse had needed to make do with one, whizzing over the second, making two more strides and leaping the third to go charging up to the corner, his head down and tail thrashing madly.

People were on their feet, cheering us on. Desperately I hauled him around to take the final changed line of obstacles. The water jump held no qualms for Dreamcatcher. I barely noticed the movement as he skimmed over it. He jarred slightly on landing but recovered, and with the commentator hollering encouragement and the crowd roaring for us to come on, come on, he made the final two jumps high and safe and kicked his heels skittishly as he left the ring to tumultuous applause.

"You've done it!" yelled Nick as I pulled up, Dreamcatcher lathered and quivering in excitement, me breathless, trembling and suddenly weak. "You've beaten the clock! Listen!"

As if from far away I heard the announcement. "First, Tessa Darcy on Dreamcatcher – and what a combination to watch for the future! Second, Nick Meredith on Rough Tweed..."

I heard no more as I flung my arms around Dream-catcher's neck and hugged him soundly, tears of happiness clouding my vision.

After that it was all a blur. Competitors gathered

around, beaming, giving their congratulations, and patting Dreamcatcher who looked smug. Mom, oblivious to the notice saying competitors only, came bursting into the collecting ring, golden curls bobbing. "Darling, you were great! I was so proud. What a fabulous horse. All that dancing he did. He was so cute I wanted to take him home!"

"Mom, I did say he was a star," I told her chokingly.

"You weren't wrong either," said Eddie, arriving ruffled and breathless from pushing his way through the throng. "Congratulations, Tessa. It was a fantastic round."

After the horses had gone through the final inspection and were pronounced sound, we were called back into the ring for the awards. Dreamcatcher with his blue rosette was practically bowing to the crowd. Rough Tweed in second place looked dignified and unfazed. Another show, another day, he seemed to be saying.

"Great job, Tessa!" said Nick yet again.

Awards given, we led the winners in a joyful lap of honor around the ring and out.

Back at the trailer, we had seen to the horses and were about to join the others in the refreshment tent when a quiet voice behind me said, "Well done, Tessa."

I spun around and came face to face with my father.

"Dad! Oh, I don't believe this! Nick, it's my dad!" My father's arms came around me and I was given the bear hug of my life. "Dad!" I whispered. "Why didn't you say you were coming?"

"I thought this way was best," he replied, setting me down gently. He looked fit and happy. His hazel eyes gleamed down at me. "That's a great little horse, Tessa. He's what used to be called a good all-arounder. Is he for sale?"

"I don't think so," said Nick at my side. That was

when it hit me that if all went according to the deal, Dreamcatcher was not for sale and never would be.

Dad looked at us inquiringly.

"It's yet to be confirmed, but we may need to discuss leasing terms," I said, wondering where his owner was, and seized by a dreadful panic in case there had been a change of mind.

Then, pushing her way through the crowds, came Jill Hardy. She pressed a bulky envelope into my hand. "Here are the roan's papers," she said smoothly, adding, "Congratulations, Tessa. You deserved the win. That clear round was fantastic. I wish you and Dreamcatcher all the very best in the future."

Almost incoherent with joy, I stammered out my thanks as the world began to spin chaotically around me. I truly had done it. Dreamcatcher was mine.

✳✳✳✳

We had yet to find out about Gyp. At the refreshment tent, Connor and Lucy explained what had happened.

"I was about to leave for the show when the phone rang," said Lucy. "It was Connor on his cell phone. The signal was terrible. I only caught snatches but I got the gist of it. He'd found Gyp in that abandoned quarry about a mile from the old lane. It's off-limits to the public because it's unsafe and the cliffs are dangerously steep. Gyp must have gone in after a stray sheep and gotten trapped. It's been three weeks. Goodness knows how he's survived all that time."

Connor said, "There was fresh spring water to drink and Gyp's more than capable of catching his own meal. I once said as much to Tessa."

"Well anyway," Lucy continued, "Connor went to the

rescue and got stuck himself. He asked me to grab Bassy and ropes to get them out. *Me!*"

"Come on, how was I supposed to know about the equine phobia?" said my stepbrother. He gave Lucy a wink, smiling. "You did it, though."

"Yes, I did, didn't I?" Lucy dimpled back at him. They looked completely friendly, as if there had been yet another magical sprinkling of golden dust. She then said, "Anyway, Bassy's such a gentle creature. No one could possibly be scared of him."

Nick and I exchanged a glance of sheer incredulity, and happiness. It was all coming out right in the end.

"We got the sheep out as well, between us," added Connor. "It was a struggle. I got accused of trying to land us all back in the quarry!"

Everyone laughed.

Topping it all was Dad's news. He had accepted the head position of the geological survey he had spoken of and was on the lookout for a house in the area.

"Maybe you'd better make it one with stabling," Mom said. She looked at me and her eyes misted. "Tessa, darling. Eddie and I have done a great deal of talking while we've been away. Today, seeing you with Dreamcatcher and everyone, has given me the push I needed. It'll be a huge sacrifice for me, Tessa, but I really think you've found your niche here. Who am I to drag you away from it?"

"We'll still be around for you, Tessa," enforced Eddie robustly. "Cross Hill is the family farm. Of course we'll be around! And rest assured, your room at the apartment will always be there when you need it. Of course, the ultimate decision rests with you."

I looked from one parent to the other, loving them

equally, wanting to be with them both. But the strange events of the summer had taught me about compromise, about options and how to move on. Mom was right. I had found my place here in Rydale.

Eddie opened some sparkling cider. Glasses were filled.

"To Dreamcatcher!" Nick said with his quirky grin.

We all raised our drinks. "Dreamcatcher!"

Our voices carried across the still-bustling venue and up into the streaky sunset. Some distance away on the old lane, a bay horse and carriage moved sedately along. The horse leaned his weight into the shafts, steady, true and forgiving. Behind, a young couple walked together hand in hand. Annie glanced up to speak to her husband, who bent his head adoringly to hers. Their talk became the glad song of birds in the hedgerow, and then they were the larks that soared up and up, until they were no more than a wisp of air above the forest, where the evening star hung bright and gleaming.

The tracks were never seen again.